MW01702144

Let's Try This Again

BUT THIS TIME IN PARIS

CYNTHIA GUNDERSON

Button Press

Chapter One

MARCH, 2014

Walter Winslow was a portly, particular man. Every morning at precisely six o'clock, he would turn off his alarm and swing his legs over the north side of the bed. He then plucked his glasses from the wooden nightstand next to him, adjusted them, and blinked approximately four times to clear his vision before standing.

His wife Wendy would reluctantly yawn in response to the disturbance she'd long grown accustomed to. Rolling over, she would pretend to be asleep until Walter disappeared into the bathroom and then fumble for her water cup on the nightstand. While she much preferred to sleep until at least half-past seven, that simply wasn't an option when married to one, Walter Winslow. Walter expected a freshly ironed shirt. Walter expected a warm breakfast before he left for the office at exactly quarter-past seven. And Walter wasn't accustomed to being disappointed.

For twenty-eight years, they'd followed the same routine.

Every night, Walter would return from the office and plop himself down in his favourite recliner and turn on old episodes of *Law and Order*, *Xena Warrior Princess*, or a handful of other American shows that Wendy had no interest in whatsoever. Even when their children were young and impressionable, she wasn't able to convince him to turn off the tube, so fat chance of that happening now that she was the only person left at home to complain. Instead of nagging, Wendy would sigh, wishing she could pick up the phone to chat with Mary —an old friend from A-levels—whilst washing the dirty dishes.

For twenty-eight years, Wendy had reluctantly resigned herself to a life of veritable boredom and predictability. But—to be fair—it wasn't *all* bad. She and Walter had plenty of good—even pleasant—moments, truly. Though, many of those moments she created with Walter actively dragging his feet. Like the day they spent at Standley Lake, or the time she insisted they take the boys to see how candy canes were made at Hammond's Candy Factory. She often wondered what those days would've looked like if he'd shown even a sliver of interest or excitement.

Even so, Walter had always provided for their family, and neither she nor their children had ever known physical want. She didn't resent him for the rest of it. At least she didn't think she did. The anger and frustration had seeped out of her years ago, replaced by an underlying level of general dissatisfaction.

Despite the fact that she had come to terms with her pragmatic existence years ago, when Wendy walked into Sprouts for her weekly produce—including ruby-red organic strawberries, since the advert listed a sale—she found herself staring unabashedly at a perfect stranger in the dairy section.

Directly in front of her, a middle-aged woman stretched

her arms to the top shelf, exposing her stomach's tanned skin as she closed her hand around a carton of whipping cream. Her jeans hugged her hips, and her hair hung freely around her shoulders, highlights from the sun somehow glinting magically in the garish light from the overhead bulbs.

Wendy tore her eyes away from the woman to glance at the cardboard container in her hand wistfully, then self-consciously adjusted the shirt over her plump midsection.

"Hello," the woman said, placing the cream in her cart. "Was I in your way?" she laughed, exposing a brilliant smile.

"N-no," Wendy stammered, blushing and shifting her weight uncomfortably. "I'm sorry, I—got distracted."

The woman waved her off, again flashing a row of perfectly straight, white teeth. "I love your accent," she said, brushing her hair off her shoulder, allowing it to swing freely behind her back. "Are you from the UK?"

"I am," Wendy answered, her cheeks blushing. "We've lived here almost nine years now, so I'm sure my accent has faded."

"It's lovely," the woman said. "What brought you to Colorado?"

"Our children," Wendy sighed, almost apologetically. It sounded like a prison sentence when she said it that way.

"Ah," the woman nodded, giving a conspiratorial wink. "My husband keeps trying to convince me to move out to California to be closer to ours, but the prices out there..." she shook her head. "That would cut into our travel budget, you know? I have my heart set on Madrid in the fall..."

Wendy's eyes opened wide with child-like wonder as she listened to the woman describe her year's plans. It was her husband's idea, she said—*her husband's idea*.

"I'm just going along for the ride, I guess. I'm sure you've seen more of the world than I have, though," the woman continued, pushing her cart further along the aisle. "We only live once, right?" She smiled again, giving a small wave as she turned the corner to the international section, taking her infectious energy and unattainable freedom with her.

Leaving her cart stranded in front of the aged gruyere, Wendy walked directly down the main aisle, turned to bypass the bulk section, and strode with purpose out the sliding glass doors to her car. With shaking hands, she turned the key in the ignition and peeled out of the parking lot faster—and with more disregard for safety—than she had ever done before in her life.

Upon arriving home that evening, Walter walked up the steps to the front door, typed in the code on the door keypad, and waited for the bolt to unlock. When the mechanical whir failed to engage, his mouth turned down in confusion, causing his tidy moustache to look more like a horseshoe of bristles hanging above his lip.

Leaning down to investigate, he gasped as a cardboard box whizzed past his head, exploding against the walkway. As Walter turned, holding a hand to his chest and breathing heavily, he blinked four times, squinting at the sight in front of him. His eyes widened in surprise when he realized that *his* wardrobe had exploded from the carton and was now strewn across the front lawn. Jumping back as another box barely missed his head, he frantically searched the air above him to discover who could possibly be ransacking their house at quarter-past six on a Wednesday.

"Take it, Walter!" Wendy hollered, her hands pressed against the windowsill and her head leaning out far enough over the roof to make eye contact. "Take it, and find somewhere else to stay tonight!"

Completely bewildered, he gawked at her in apoplectic shock, his jaw hanging slack. And that is precisely how one, Walter Winslow, ended up flat on his back amid his rumpled clothing on his own immaculately manicured lawn.

Chapter Two

"Walt," Wendy said for the fifteenth time, cradling his head in her lap and running a wet cloth across his forehead.

Walter groaned, his eyelids fluttering as he lifted his sluggish arms off the grass.

"Wendy?" he said, looking up at his dear wife of twenty-eight years. "What happ—" he started to say, but then—noticing the textile explosion surrounding his legs—his lips drew into a thin line. Slowly sitting up, he brushed off his trousers and turned to face the woman who nearly took his head off with a cardboard projectile.

"Wendy, I'm perplexed," he said, attempting to be as diplomatic as possible. "Have I done something wrong—"

Before he could finish his sentence, Wendy launched herself—nearly jumping into his lap—her chest heaving with deep, wracking sobs. Walter sat there, his arms at his sides, in complete befuddlement. Though Wendy had been emotional at times during their marriage—mainly when he left milk on the table or forgot to turn his trousers right-side-out before putting them in the laundry bin—this was behavior he had never witnessed.

She quickly pulled away, kneeling regretfully in the grass and wiping the tears from her splotchy cheeks.

"Wendy," he tried again, "why is half my wardrobe littered across our lawn? And did I hear you correctly? You'd like me to 'Take it, and find somewhere else to stay tonight?'"

Wendy sighed, her shoulders slumping, still not able to meet his eyes.

"Walt, I'm sorry about your clothes and—and all this mess," she said, motioning to the yard around her. Slow tears leaked down her cheeks as she continued, "But I'm not sorry about what I said. For twenty-eight years, I've been here. In this house," she said, her voice building in energy as she pointed toward the front door. "I've cooked, I've cleaned, I've done the laundry, I've raised our children, and—" she paused, sucking in a deep breath, "—not *once* have you asked me what I'd like to do in life. Not *once* have you asked me where *I'd* like to go for dinner or whether *I'd* like to plan a holiday or what *my* dreams are or—"

"Wendy—"

"No, Walter, let me finish!" she cut in, her voice nearly hysterical.

Walter flinched at the intensity of her tone, and the accusatory finger pointed directly at his chest.

"I loved you, Walt—at least I loved the way I thought love was supposed to be, but...I don't know if it was love! Was it? In the beginning, definitely, but that was a long time ago. It seems like that love should have grown or become fuller. It should feel...like *more*, you know? I haven't been happy—"

"Haven't been happy—"

"No, Walt! I've been *fine*. Just fine! But *I'd like to go to Madrid*!" Wendy shouted. "And I'd like to not have to fight for it!"

"My id—Madrid?" Walter blustered, throwing his hands in the air. "You've never mentioned Madrid—"

"Or whatever! That's an example, for goodness sake. I would love you to have any idea that would make our life more full, more colorful. I'd like to see the world! To try new foods, meet new people, find out what *I* love—what makes me feel alive and free and—"

"Wendy, did something happen while you were out?" Walter asked, lifting a hand to her forehead. "Did someone give you something—a little pill, or a drink or something—"

"NO, WALTER!" Wendy shouted, slapping him away.

"The thing is," Walter said, holding up his arms in defense, "I've never heard you say anything like this in your life! All this—this talk about running around for no purpose? I've never heard—"

"You've never asked," Wendy said, her voice low. "I want a divorce, Walter."

Walter's eyes widened in shock. "A *divorce*?"

"That's what I said," she sniffed. "A divorce. I'm done acting for everyone else. I want to actually live before this," she gestured at her body, "breaks down and I have no living left in me."

"But Wendy, the children—"

"Don't 'but Wendy' me, Walt. The children have their own lives. They don't need mum and dad to hold their hands anymore."

Wendy gingerly lifted herself from the lawn, brushed herself off, and climbed the front doorsteps.

"You don't have to stay somewhere else," she said softly. "I'll take the guest room."

With that, she walked through the front door and left Walter alone with his clothes.

Though Wendy had offered to take the guest room, Walter understood correctly that this was not the time to take her at her word. He insisted on moving to the room that used to belong to their two boys. Though the bunk beds were gone, he could still see the slightly darker outline on the pale blue paint where the frame had blocked sunlight from hitting the wall.

Already in his cotton pajamas, he pulled down the twin bed's quilt and top-sheet and rolled onto the mattress. It felt odd to be in a new room. He never slept away from Wendy—besides a handful of nights when Wendy was off on a school trip with one of the boys, or he was at a conference.

That had been years ago. Owning his accounting firm for the last eight years meant there was no requirement to travel anymore. Honestly, that had been his primary motivation for striking out on his own. He didn't enjoy being forced into networking dinners or continuing education events—why did we have the internet if not to avoid awkward social gatherings like those?

Walter had assumed Wendy was grateful their lives had settled down when he opened shop, but now...He lay there , flipping the sheets loosely over himself, and resting his hands on his ample belly. What *did* he know about Wendy? Had all of these thoughts been bouncing around her head for years, and he'd never noticed? He pondered this, staring at the ceiling as if hoping to find some bit of wisdom there. Eventually, he forced his eyes closed and began to breathe deeply—willing his anxious body to sleep.

Within minutes, he abruptly threw off the sheets and lowered his restless legs to the floor. Walking to the window, he flicked the latches open and slid the glass pane to the left, allowing the night air to flow freely into the room. Gripping the sill, he breathed in, his chest expanding and filling with the fresh scent of the pine tree next to the house.

His eyebrows furrowed as his mind raced with questions, none of which had satisfying answers. Nothing Wendy'd said made any sense to him, and that felt terrifying. What could Wendy possibly be thinking? Divorce at this age would be impractical and expensive, not to mention incredibly time-consuming and disruptive. What had her experience been all these years, and how had it been so opposite from what he interpreted? Why hadn't she said anything? How was it his responsibility to become a mind-reader and intuitively know there was a problem? As his thoughts buzzed, one line played over and over in his head: 'I loved you, Walter.' Loved, not love.

His lip began to tremble as he stared above the houses. Quickly flicking away a tear that had sneakily slipped to his cheek, he closed the window resolutely and returned reluctantly to his bed for the night.

Chapter Three

At breakfast the next morning, Walter couldn't decide where to look. Wendy had prepared eggs, fried tomatoes, and toast, which only made him more anxious than he had been the night before. It seemed too ordinary. If he didn't feel like a truck had plowed him over, he could've easily been convinced that the night before was all a bad dream.

Even with his late-night and lack of alarm, he had awakened at exactly six o'clock. He had tip-toed carefully into his bedroom and found it empty. Except for the clean, ironed shirt draped over the bedpost. It seemed like a dangerous omen. He showered and dressed, just as he always had, but everything felt different. Fragile.

"Thank you," he said, snapping back to the moment as Wendy set the plate on the table in front of him. He briefly attempted to meet her eyes, but quickly settled on staring at his plate instead. Had he said 'thank you' for yesterday's breakfast, he wondered? Not sure whether to begin eating or wait for her to join him, he sat still with his hands folded in his lap. Without a word, Wendy set the frying pan in the sink and walked back up the stairs, closing their bedroom door with gusto.

Walter's gaze followed her, his expression blank. Then, picking up his knife, he carefully cut his toast, egg, and tomato into bite-sized pieces. Placing one forkful after another in his mouth, he chewed and swallowed until the plate was clean. Pushing his chair away from the table, he stood and walked toward the front door to collect his briefcase. Before leaning over to grip the leather handle, he paused and turned back toward the kitchen. Slowly, he retraced his steps to the table, picked up his plate and utensils, and carried them to the sink.

"You did *what*?" Mary exclaimed on the other end of the line.

"I know," Wendy sighed, leaning against the kitchen counter.

"You actually tossed his clothes out the window?"

"I did," she admitted, closing her eyes and holding her palm to her forehead.

"How'd old Walt take that bit of excitement?"

"He fainted dead away. Landed in the lawn."

Mary laughed, and Wendy couldn't help but laugh with her.

"I bet he did," Mary muttered.

"The thing is, he seemed completely shocked. Like he hadn't a clue I'd been unhappy all these years!" Wendy said, trapping the phone between her ear and shoulder as she turned to pull the plates from the drying rack.

"Men," Mary sighed, a baby crying in the background.

"Is Clara over?" Wendy asked.

"She is. I'm looking after her on Thursdays now."

"Three days a week. That's a big commitment," Wendy said, placing the last plate in the cupboard.

"She's a love," Mary said. "And it won't be for long. Her mum's finishing up her program in just over a month."

"I keep waiting for Calvin to call and tell me they're expecting," Wendy said.

"Do you think they're having trouble?"

"I don't know, honestly. Becky's a bit sensitive, especially where I'm concerned."

"Ah. Well, you've still got a few good years left before you're truly grandmother material," Mary said, and Wendy grinned, walking into the sitting room and settling on the sofa.

"What will you do?" Mary asked softly.

"No clue, Mar," Wendy answered, leaning her head against the cushion. "I just knew at that moment that I had to...do something. I haven't thought past that."

"I think it's brilliant," Mary said. "You've been stuck for far too long. Ooh! You could make a list of all the things you've ever wanted to do and start checking them off."

"I could," Wendy said hesitantly. "I wouldn't even know where to start, I'm afraid."

"That's simple. Go to your desk, pick up a pen and a piece of paper—are you going?" Mary asked, waiting to hear proof of Wendy's obedience.

"Yes, alright," Wendy laughed, shifting on the couch, but remaining seated.

"You've got it?"

"Yes," she lied, pretending to be taking notes.

"Perfect. On the top, list 'places,' 'experiences,' 'skills,' and...I don't know, just make a separate column for each category. List everything; it doesn't have to be practical. You can go through them again later. It's called a mind sweep."

Wendy again heard the baby in the background.

"Wonderful," Wendy said, smiling. "I'll work on this today. Sounds like you need to go."

"I want to hear what you come up with."

"I promise. I'll call you tomorrow."

After hanging up, Wendy stretched her legs across the sofa and lay flat against the cushions. Closing her eyes, she pulled a throw blanket over her body and promptly fell asleep.

Chapter Four

"You're serious," Walter said quietly, sitting across from Wendy at the kitchen table.

Wendy nodded, drawing small, swirly loops around the words 'Wednesday, three o'clock' that she'd written earlier on the notepad.

"How did you find this lawyer?"

"Mary's friend—"

"Of course it would be Mary," Walter muttered.

"What's that supposed to mean?" Wendy asked, folding her arms across her chest.

"Nothing," Walter sighed, smoothing his moustache. "I don't think she's ever cared for me, that's all."

"She likes you just fine," Wendy huffed. "She only gave me the information because I asked."

Walter stared at Wendy's doodling, sitting up with a little more confidence as an idea began to percolate in his mind.

"What do you want to do?" he asked.

"What do you mean—?

"I mean, what have you been desperate to do that you haven't done over the last—well, since whenever you started feeling unhappy? And how long have you felt that way, by the way?"

"I don't think I could put an exact date on it," Wendy said haughtily.

"I think it would just be helpful for me to know when this started—"

"It started from the beginning!" Wendy said, exasperated. "But back then, all of the excitement and busyness made it less obvious. Then it grew and grew, and now it's this big thing—" Wendy attempted to explain, but upon seeing Walter's skeptical expression, she stopped mid-sentence.

"I'm sorry," Walter said. "I simply don't understand."

"That's kind of the point," Wendy breathed. Blinking at him, she paused for a moment before answering his other questions.

"I made a list," she answered finally.

"A list!" Walter exclaimed sincerely as if this was the first thing that computed from the entire conversation. "Let's take a look."

"You want to see it?" Wendy asked hesitantly.

Walter motioned for her to put it on the table, and she stood to retrieve it from the counter.

"I wrote down everything—I don't think I'll be able to do them all, but Mar—" she cleared her throat. "Well, I thought it would be a good idea to write everything down and go through it later."

Walter nodded, pulling the paper toward him. Wendy blushed as she watched his eyes scan across the lengthy list.

"Scuba diving?" he said, raising an eyebrow.

Wendy twisted and untwisted a napkin between her fingers. "I've never seen a coral reef with my own eyes."

"There are plenty of ways to see a reef without taking on the risk of blowing an eardrum. Snorkeling would be more—"

"Practical, I know," she said, looking down at the table.

Walter tapped his finger on the table as he watched her shrink at his comment. He swallowed hard. Returning his gaze to the paper in front of him, he noticed one column with a single entry.

"Paris?" he asked, looking up at his wife.

"Mmhmm," she nodded, still not meeting his eyes.

"But you've been to Paris," he said, leaning back in his chair.

"No, Walter, *you've* been to Paris. I sat in the hotel room with a three-month-old attached to my breast as I stared out the window, *wishing* I could see Paris."

"But we went for dinner—"

"Eating in the hotel dining room does *not* count as a cultural experience."

Walter nodded. "I...know I'm not the most exciting chap," he began, leaning his arms on the table, "and I'm trying to understand, but I thought—our life has been good, hasn't it? We had a real romance back in the day, didn't we?"

"We did," Wendy whispered, a sad smile lifting the edges of her lips. "But that's the problem, Walt. It ended a long time ago. And I'm not saying it's all your fault, either. I was so overwhelmed with babies and housekeeping, and then the busyness and stress of having teens, and then moving to a new country and trying desperately to tether myself to the boys' lives," she said, her voice breaking. "After all that...I don't know who I am. And I don't think I know who you are anymore either."

"I'm the same person I've always been—"

"Walt," she cut in, raising an eyebrow. "You took me to Alton Towers on our third date and rode the Corkscrew."

Walt laughed out loud, slapping his hand on his thigh. "I was trying to impress you!"

"It was not impressive; it was terrifying. And don't tell me it was all for my benefit. I was the one urging you not to listen to your mates."

Walter shrugged his shoulders. The moment of levity passed too quickly, and the grin slipped from his face. He began to fiddle with the pen Wendy had left next to the notepad.

"What if...we got to know each other again?" he asked nervously. "I could try to be different—"

"Walt," she said gently. "I don't want you to have to *be* someone different. I think we just *are* different at this point. We've both stagnated for so long, and now...I want something new."

"But what if I don't," he said, looking up at her boldly. "What if I still love you, and...I didn't know you wanted more —I foolishly believed we were happy—and now that I know, I'd like to try—"

"I think it's too late," Wendy whispered abruptly, standing and walking to the cupboard, retrieving two glasses, and filling them with water from the dispenser on the door of the fridge. Setting one in front of Walter, she again took her seat.

"But how's that fair, Wendy? You've never said a thing for —for nearly thirty years, and now, I find out you have all these dreams and thoughts and such...and you're not even going to give me a chance?"

"I have said things!" Wendy erupted, slamming her hands on the table. "Remember that time when I told you I'd like to apply for a hospital job?"

Stymied, Walter desperately searched his memory.

"You told me that wasn't 'practical' because there were nights I wouldn't be home to make dinner, and we 'didn't need more income' and 'perhaps I could look for a hobby that got me home in the afternoon,'" Wendy said.

"I don't remember that," Walter blustered, "I recall you saying you wanted to volunteer at the food bank—"

"Only because you wouldn't support me in what I wanted! That wasn't even my second or third choice, but it was something that got me out of the house and gave me some sort of—purpose!"

"Well, why didn't you say something?" Walter argued. "If I would've known you felt so strongly about it—"

"Walter, that's the point. I shouldn't have to prove myself for you to be on board. I want a partner who's looking for opportunities to help me spread my wings. Not one who is so uncomfortable with progress that he purposefully clips them."

Walter reeled back as if she'd slapped him. Speechless, he stared at her, hurt written all over his face.

"Walt, I—"

"No," he said, stopping her with a raised hand. Beads of sweat began forming on his forehead, and he clenched and unclenched his fingers and toes to keep the blood flowing. It would be too big of an ego hit to pass out twice in front of Wendy in a week.

He stared at the tabletop, attempting to sort through the weighty information he'd been forced to ingest. If Wendy was on point, he was coming smack up against the fact that he'd unwittingly been torpedoing his marriage for years. And if hers was a revisionist history...well, it didn't matter, did it? She felt how she felt and arguing the facts wasn't going to change that at this point.

With shaking limbs and in a sudden burst of spontaneity, Walter stood up, adjusted his belt, and looked intently at his wife.

"What if I came with you?" he said resolutely.

"Came with me—where exactly?"

"To Paris."

"I don't even know what I'm doing yet," Wendy countered, "and if I do go, I'm not planning to only be there for a week, or even two. I think I might...move there."

"Permanently?"

"I don't know! This is all so new; I'm simply brainstorming."

"What if I moved with you?" he said, placing his hands on his hips.

Wendy raised an eyebrow. "You can't take your practice to Paris," she said, mildly amused.

"I'm well aware," he said. "But we've got savings, and I could give Patrick an advance to run the place—"

"You aren't serious—"

"I'm deadly serious," he insisted.

"Walt, you despise traveling—especially if long plane rides are involved—and what would you even do there?"

"I'd be with you! I'd do whatever you were doing!"

"No, you're not hearing me," Wendy said, standing up, her hands balled into fists at her sides. "I can't take care of you anymore, Walter! I need my own space—to figure out who I am and what I want out of life. When you're here—ugh!" she groaned in frustration. "I've spent so many years worrying about what you want and what pleases you that I can't stop. I feel this—this responsibility and pressure to make sure you're happy and comfortable. If you were with me in Paris, it wouldn't *be* Paris for me," she said in a rush, her body tense.

Walter flinched, each of her words stinging more than the last as they flew like daggers across the table. Wendy stood in silence, breathing heavily. Pursing his lips, he marched past her and up the stairs to the guest room.

"The appointment's on Wednesday," she called after him, her words barely hitting his ears before he slammed the door.

Chapter Five

The next morning, Wendy did not get up and make breakfast. She slept in until half-past seven as she had always dreamed of doing on a weekday, and it felt glorious. Walking down to the kitchen in her pajamas, she was surprised to find Walter's dishes clean and drying in the rack. She stretched her arms high above her head, smiling at the beam of sunlight streaming through the kitchen window and the utter quiet surrounding her.

Taking her time, she pulled yogurt from the fridge, granola from the cupboard, and sliced the last of the strawberries she'd purchased at Sprouts the other day. A perfect breakfast for a perfectly lovely morning. All she could think about as she ate was that woman at the grocery store—the intoxicating air of energy, excitement, and freedom that surrounded her. Wendy became more determined than ever to find that confidence for herself. To be excited about waking up in the morning, to say yes to all the things Walter had said no to over the years. This was her time, and she wasn't going to waste it.

After leaving her dishes in the sink—unwashed—she snatched the cloth from the sink and gave the table a perfunctory once-over, then hustled up the stairs to her bedroom to get dressed. She quickly slipped on her most colorful blouse—the one that Walter said showed too much of her bosom—and pulled on her favorite trousers. After washing her face, she applied mascara and swiped her lips with a fresh tube of bright pink lipstick, then grabbed her purse from the nightstand and headed for the door.

Wendy nearly skipped down the street toward the food bank; the sunshine and birds chattering to each other in the trees only validated her current mood. When she arrived at the door, she hesitated—her hand resting on the handle. Taking a deep breath, she pulled it open and walked resolutely through the airlock, her hair blowing in the sudden burst of air conditioning. With her head held high, she marched up to the intake desk.

"I need to resign," she announced to the young man seated behind the counter.

"Resign?" he asked, a look of confusion on his face.

"Yes, I volunteer here on Tuesdays," she explained.

"Ah," he said, "that explains why I've never met you. I only volunteer Friday through Sunday."

"Yes, well, as I said. I would like to terminate my position."

"Okay," he said hesitantly, "I can give you a post-it note and then give it to Mark when he comes in this afternoon."

"A post-it?" Wendy asked, scandalized by the casual suggestion. "Don't I need to fill out some paperwork or...sign something?"

The young man chuckled, "No, we're not that intense around here. If you aren't able to volunteer anymore, you can just leave Mark a note. Or, if you want to give me your name, I can let him know. Either way."

"But I've volunteered here every week for almost three years. Don't you think they'll need some time to fill that position?"

"Oh, you'll be missed, definitely, but we'll shuffle some things around. You don't need to worry or anything," he said, nodding and grinning like...well, like a young man.

"Alright, then," Wendy said, turning slowly from the desk. "My name is Wendy Winslow," she said, walking toward the exit.

"I'll let him know, thanks for coming in!" the man called after her.

Wendy waved without giving a backward glance.

The next morning was Saturday, which meant Walter was home. Wendy recognized this immediately when she opened her eyes after waking to a clatter in the kitchen downstairs. Glancing at the clock on her nightstand, she saw that it was nearly eight o'clock in the morning.

She jumped out of bed, quickly changing into three-quarter length joggers and a t-shirt. The night before, she had set her barely-utilized trainers and a pair of athletic socks near the door. Finding her list on the dresser, she picked up a pencil and drew a big check-mark next to the line 'begin a new exercise routine' before picking up her shoes and opening the door.

"Good morning," Walter said cheerily, greeting her as she descended the stairs. "Off for a walk?"

Wendy inspected the scene before her: Walter, in *jeans*—was she aware he even owned jeans?—whisking something together in a large bowl with sausages frying on the stove. When he looked in her direction—his hand still mixing—she nodded.

"Breakfast will be ready when you get back," he said simply, turning again to his task.

Pinching herself, she walked toward the front door and attempted to slip her shoes on. They were much too snug at first, but after loosening the laces, she was able to get them on without a fight.

Wendy walked down the steps, looked both directions, and set off in a random direction at a brisk pace. Within seconds it seemed, her breathing quickened, and her heart began to pound in her chest. How long had it been since she'd done something purposefully active? It's not like she spent her days sitting on the couch and watching the telly, but her body was clearly not used to moving this fast.

Refusing to give in to the discomfort, she pushed forward down the street, and eventually, her breathing settled into a more comfortable rhythm. She walked approximately two miles away from the house before realizing that she hadn't gone in a loop as intended and instead needed to turn back and return the way she had come.

Arriving back at the house—though she was positive she looked like a gigantic ripe tomato—she proudly stepped through the door and walked into the kitchen for a drink. She'd been gone long enough that Walter was no longer waiting, but he had set a plate on the table for her. Two hotcakes, two sausages, and a fried egg stared up at her as she gulped down the cold water.

Glancing through the window in the back door, she found Walter pulling weeds along the fence. A small twinge of guilt pricked her heart, but she shook her head, took a deep breath, then sat down to enjoy the first breakfast she hadn't had to cook for herself in a long time.

With her hair still in a towel from the shower, Wendy rushed to pick up the phone.

"Hallo?" she said, slightly out of breath.

"Morning, mum," Calvin greeted her. "How are you and Dad getting along?"

Wendy froze.

"Are you there?" Calvin asked.

"Yes, sorry, I'm here. I just got out of the shower. We're doing fine."

"Well, I won't keep you. I was calling to see if Becky and I could visit you two next weekend," he said, clearly anticipating a positive response.

"That would be wonderful," Wendy exclaimed, her face lighting up. "What prompted this?"

"Nothing specific. I have a few days off and we thought it would be fun to pop in."

"Are you able to get decent flights?"

"Yes, mum," he laughed. "Nonstop from San Francisco to Denver, arriving...at 8:05 PM next Friday. Does that work?"

"That'd be lovely. Leaving Sunday, I assume?"

"Right, I have to get back for Monday."

"We'd be glad to have you," Wendy gushed. "I'll ring Darrel and see if he's able to get away."

"Tell him we get the bedroom," Calvin teased, and Wendy laughed.

"We'll figure it out. I've got that air mattress he can use," she said.

"See you next week, Mum."

"Looking forward to it," Wendy said, holding the receiver for a moment after Calvin hung up. Placing the phone back in its dock, Wendy pulled the towel from her head and hung it up in the bathroom, then reached for her hairbrush.

"Who was on the line?" Walter asked, and Wendy jumped, dropping the brush and yelping in pain as it struck her pinky toe.

"I'm sorry, darling," Walter said, reaching for the brush. "I didn't mean to frighten you. I was just coming in to shower—I got quite dirty working in the yard."

Wendy wiped the tears from her eyes and took a cleansing breath. "Thanks for breakfast," she said, watching Walter's eyes shine with pride at her acknowledgment.

"You're welcome," he said, clearing his throat.

"That was Calvin. He and Becky want to come out for a visit next weekend."

"That's unexpected," Walter said, smiling.

"I know, he said he had a few days off. I think I'll ring Darrel and see if he's able to join us."

"Just for the weekend?"

"Mmhmm," Wendy answered, taking the brush from Walter's outstretched hand and running it through her damp hair. Noticing Walter's silence, she glanced at him. His eyebrows were pulled together in concern.

"What is it?" she asked.

"Oh, nothing, I...was just thinking about sleeping arrangements," he said, a blush rising to his cheeks.

Wendy nodded slowly. "I don't want to tell the boys yet, Walt. Let's have a nice visit, and we can decide what to do after."

"So that means..."

"Yes, we'll sleep in here, and Calvin and Becky can take the boys' room. We can pull out the air mattress for Darrel."

Walter nodded.

"I'll get out of the way so you can shower."

"Do you need to dry your hair?" Walter asked.

"I'll take the dryer to the powder room," she said, reaching for the cord and pulling it from the outlet.

Chapter Six

MARCH, 1980

"C'mon, Wendy," Mary pleaded. "It'll be fun, I promise."

"I'm not worried about the fun; I'm worried about the studying that won't be accomplished whilst the 'fun' is occurring!" Wendy complained.

"You're always studying," Mary muttered. "You're seventeen. Live a little!" she cajoled, pulling Wendy off of her bed, nearly toppling her textbooks on the floor.

"Mary, I'm always studying because this stuff is difficult for me. I don't have posh parents to bail me out."

"Neither do I—"

"But it comes easier to you, and don't try to argue that point."

Mary rolled her eyes. "I don't know why you're so set on having a big career. Just marry rich. That's my plan."

Wendy laughed as Mary wrapped a scarf around her neck and strutted across the room.

"How long are we going to be there?" Wendy asked, her eyes serious.

"Not a minute past ten, I promise," Mary answered hopefully.

"You promise..."

"I swear it," Mary pleaded. Seeing Wendy's face begin to soften, she jumped up and down exuberantly, "Oh thank you so much! I've been dying to meet up with Lucy's mates, but I couldn't bear the thought of going alone—"

"Alright, alright!" Wendy said, interrupting Mary's prattling. "Let's get this over with."

As the two girls entered the crowded pub, they were immediately waved over to a booth by Lucy—or at least that's who Wendy assumed she was. Mary had talked about her cousin fondly and had expounded regularly on her sense of fashion. Tonight, Lucy's permed hair, overly wide belt around a loose sweater, and mini leather skirt didn't disappoint. Wendy couldn't help but stare at the thin stitch of clothing around her thighs, wondering if they were going to see more than they bargained for if she bent over.

"Luc, this is my friend Wendy," Mary shouted, leaning in to be heard over the hubbub. "We can't stay for long, but thought we'd stop by."

"Glad you did," Lucy said with a broad smile. "There's still room for a few more," she said, motioning for her mates to shift over to make space for the newcomers.

As Wendy took a seat, squishing in next to Mary, she glanced at the other faces around the table and gasped in surprise. The large, circular booth was filled with blokes. She hadn't noticed that when they'd initially walked in. It was Lucy and six strapping young men, all staring directly at her and Mary. Wendy gulped.

"Mary, Wendy, these are my mates from the Academy.

Tim, Kelly, Nathan, Ron, Matthew, and Walter," Lucy announced jovially.

"When you told me who you were out with, I assumed Kelly was a girl," Mary admitted sheepishly.

"I get that a lot," Kelly laughed, taking a crisp from one of the plates on the table piled high with pub food.

"Pleased to meet you," Wendy said with a small wave, suddenly extremely self-conscious.

Lucy and Mary began naturally conversing with Tim and Kelly, but as they were facing slightly away from Wendy, she couldn't quite make out what they were saying. She strained to hear and somehow participate in the conversation, but wasn't having much luck. Not wanting to look left out, she reached for food to put on her empty plate.

"How do you know Lucy?" a voice said from across the table, catching her attention. She turned to face him and caught her breath. The boy seated across from her was handsome. His soft brown eyes gazed at her, preventing her from inspecting his slightly tousled hair or loosely buttoned Oxford shirt.

"Hmm?" she stalled, swallowing hard.

"How d'you know Lucy?" he asked again, leaning toward her.

"Ah," she nodded, pretending to just now hear his question. "I actually don't, if I'm honest. Mary's my best friend, and she also happens to be Lucy's cousin. I'm just along for the ride tonight, I'm afraid," she said with a laugh. "Remind me, your name—?"

"Walter," he said. "I'm kind of in the same boat, but—well, I've known Lucy for years. But I'm not typically available for this kind of socialization."

Wendy cocked her head to the side. "What do you mean?"

"They all accuse me of being too serious about my studies, but I'd never describe it that way. I'm playing the long-game."

Wendy laughed, "Is that so?"

"It is! I'm simply practical. If I study now, I'll have plenty of time to engage in frivolity later—but I'll have money to spend and a family to enjoy it with."

"Mary had to pull me away from my books to get me here," Wendy admitted conspiratorially. "She promised me we'd leave no later than ten, so I can get back to it."

Walter grinned. "Ah! Finally. A woman after my own heart."

Wendy blushed.

"Well, if we're both stuck here 'till ten, let's at least eat some of this so we won't be hungry for studying later, shall we?" Walter said.

"Agreed," Wendy answered, her face flushed as Walter stretched his arm near hers to pick up a plate.

At half-past eleven, Wendy and Mary finally burst back through the door of Mary's house. Luckily, Wendy was staying the weekend there, or her parents would've had a fit at seeing her return after curfew. Mary motioned for Wendy to quietly close the door and follow her down the hall to her room, so as not to wake her mum who'd already gone to bed for the night.

They quickly changed, washed their faces, and brushed their teeth, and then flopped onto Mary's bed as soon as Wendy could move her textbooks out of the way. Though physically tired, their minds were abuzz with energy from their unsanctioned evening out.

"Did you see Ron's tattoo?" Mary whispered excitedly.

"No! Where was it? And when did that happen?" Wendy giggled.

"He showed it to us after we got our sandwiches, remember?"

Wendy shook her head slowly.

"Ugh," Mary groaned. "You were probably talking to that fellow on the end—you do realize you gabbed with him all night?"

"Not all night—"

"All night, Wendy! Ron took his arm out of his shirt and everything—it was on the back of his shoulder. You honestly missed it?"

"I don't remember seeing any bare shoulders," Wendy laughed, and Mary quickly shushed her.

"Well, what on earth was so important that you couldn't be bothered by glistening bare skin and bulging muscles—"

Wendy hit Mary with a pillow. "There weren't any bulging muscles on Ron, and I could tell that without seeing him with his shirt off!" Wendy teased as Mary tossed the pillow back on her lap, attempting to laugh as quietly as possible.

"Fair," she sighed. "But seriously, Wendy, what were you two talking about?"

"Nothing, really," she shrugged. "His name's Walter. We just had a lot in common, I guess."

"He wasn't *that* cute," Mary said.

"Was too!" Wendy said a little too loudly, and Mary clamped a hand over her mouth. "You're just jealous," she whispered when Mary finally set her free. "He likes studying, too, which means he's definitely got the best chance of success in that group."

Mary rolled her eyes. "Not likely. And I had five others to choose from," she said, waggling her eyebrows.

Wendy rolled her eyes and dropped to the floor, pulling a mat from under Mary's bed. "We can discuss this further in the morning, but I've got to get to bed. You promised me an early night, remember?" she said, feigning annoyance.

"You little—I asked you if you wanted to leave, and you said—" Mary started, but was quickly cut off with another pillow flying toward her face.

Chapter Seven

APRIL, 2014

On Sunday, Monday, and Tuesday before the boys' arrival, Wendy spent hours going through closets and cupboards, making piles of everything she couldn't see herself needing in Paris. Or ever, for that matter. She'd held on to knick-knacks and old clothing, picnic blankets, and puzzles, all in the hopes that someday she'd find a use for them when grandchildren came along. Looking at them now, she had an overwhelming desire to light it all on fire.

After taking multiple trips to the local thrift store, she had only two piles left. One was the pile of things Walter removed from her original donation piles, and one was left for Calvin and Darrel to go through. Anything they wanted, they could keep, but the rest she'd truck off to the ARC.

She understood why Walter wanted to keep the things he did, and it didn't impact her life at this point. Eventually, they'd be living in separate homes, and she could keep hers as decluttered as she liked. Their appointment was in an hour, and Wendy hoped the lawyer would be able to help them figure out what came next. After talking with Mary, she already knew it would be a long, drawn-out process, but hopefully, they could make it slightly less complicated by agreeing on a plan beforehand.

Wendy was sitting at the kitchen table eating apple slices when the front door swung open. Walter was surprisingly willing to take a few hours off work to make this meeting. She turned to see him set his briefcase next to the coat rack and place his shoes on the mat.

"I'll go change," he said brusquely, heading for the stairs.

"We've still got a few minutes before we need to leave," she reminded him, but he didn't turn to acknowledge her comment.

She sighed, standing and taking her plate to the sink. They hadn't said much to each other over the last few days, but the saddest part about that situation was how utterly normal it felt. How long had it been since they'd had a real conversation? Besides the one about getting divorced.

Wendy meant what she'd said that night—she didn't know Walter anymore. Besides watching him watch the telly, she hadn't a clue what made him happy in life. That couldn't be what a real, thriving relationship was. Weren't they supposed to do things for each other? Talk late into the night about their hopes and dreams? Go have adventures together? She knew it wasn't practical to live life like that every single day, but it would be nice to feel close every once in a while. That wasn't too much to expect, was it?

She took a deep breath, plucked her handbag from the coat rack, and walked out to the front step. Sitting on the wooden stair, she pulled her knees to her chest and wrapped her arms around them. How *was* a good relationship supposed to look? Thinking about it now, she couldn't think of one example in real life, and she doubted characters in Jane Austen novels counted.

Mary divorced Bruce years ago and hadn't ever remarried, though she'd had a few noteworthy beaus. Wendy's own parents—though they stayed together 'till the day her father passed—weren't models of how to create the marital energy or passion she felt she lacked. How was she supposed to know what to shoot for? *What type of relationship would truly make her happy?*

"Shall we be off, then?" Walter said, stepping out the front door.

Wendy jumped, standing up abruptly. "Yes, let's."

"I'll drive," Walter said matter-of-factly, then hesitated with the keys in his hand. "Unless...would you prefer to take the wheel?"

"No, that's fine," Wendy sighed. "Thanks for asking, though," she said, her eyes briefly meeting his before she quickly looked away.

"Your blouse is...summery," Walter said awkwardly as they walked to the driveway. "It matches your eyes."

Wendy blushed in spite of herself. "Thank you," she said, gripping the passenger door handle of their Lexus crossover and pulling.

Both seated in the car, Walter pressed the start button and pulled onto the street. Being in such close physical proximity to each other made the distance between them palpable. Driving from Broomfield to Arvada meant a solid twenty-five minutes in the car together and, after looking out the window for seven of those minutes, Wendy finally broke the silence.

"Thank you for coming home to do this. I hope it won't mess up the rest of your workweek," she said timidly.

"Couldn't skip out on my marriage ending, now could I?" Walter said with a low, derisive laugh.

"Walt—" Wendy started but didn't finish her sentence. She had high hopes for this being a civil separation, but now she wasn't so sure. She turned again to gaze past the glass at the passing landscape. There wasn't anything to say to that. Suddenly, Walter veered onto a side street, and the change in momentum slammed Wendy uncomfortably into the door.

"Walter, what in the—"

"Just hold on," he muttered, fastidiously inspecting the landscape in front of him as he drove.

After a few more disruptive twists and turns, Walter finally pulled to a stop in a mostly empty dirt parking lot.

"What are you doing, Walter?" Wendy asked, scanning their surroundings.

"I thought you loved Standley. Remember that time—" Walter started, but Wendy held up a hand as he unbuckled his seatbelt.

Wendy shook her head, pulling in a cleansing breath. The nerve he had bringing her here, as if he hadn't thrown a fit when she proposed a day-trip at this very spot years ago. And to pretend he had happy memories on top of it?

"This is quite possibly the worst place you could've taken me today, Walt, and we have an appointment to keep—"

"Google Maps says we're twenty minutes early and this is on the way," he said, opening the car door and stepping out. "Would you come along with me for a short walk?"

Wendy fumed in her seat, but eventually joined him in the lot. "I don't want to be late—"

"I know, this'll only take a few moments," he said kindly, motioning for her to follow. Walter led her to a path that wound toward the lake, then split in opposite directions to wrap around the large body of water. She hadn't worn the best shoes for walking, but thankfully the path wasn't particularly rocky or muddy. As she approached his side, Walter reached for her hand. She instinctively pulled away.

Walter pursed his lips, his moustache bunching up beneath his nose. "The thing is," he said, pausing and turning toward her. "You don't want to be married anymore, and I've done a lot of thinking," he said in a rush, clasping his hands behind his back. "The very idea of that...I was completely gobsmacked if I'm being honest, and I'm still attempting to make sense of everything you've told me over the past week," he said, gazing pensively at the trees above them. "Truth be told, I haven't been wholly focused on our relationship, but it wasn't *purposeful*, Wendy. I didn't know how you were feeling and I just got...I dunno, lazy, I guess."

Wendy nodded, noticing the irregular shimmer in his eyes and his excessive blinking.

"So," Walter continued, "I have a proposal. A compromise, so to speak. I would like to stay married to you, and you have set your mind on the opposite, so I thought: what if we met in the middle?"

Wendy's brow lowered. "I don't think we can be...partly married, Walter," she said, placing a hand on her hip.

"No, definitely not, but what if we agreed on a trial. On a timeline. With rules."

"I've never heard of such a thing," she huffed.

"Neither have I," Walter admitted, "but who says we can't do something different? Try something new, as you described the other night."

She eyed him skeptically. "This is very unlike you, Walter."

"You, yourself, said you don't feel like you know me and that I don't know you, so perhaps this is exactly like me, and you just don't know it," he said stubbornly.

Wendy sighed, dropping her hand and walking to sit on a wooden bench a few meters away, near the rushes at the edge of the lake.

"Hunky-dory," she said sarcastically, "What would these rules be exactly?"

"I haven't put much thought into it, honestly. The idea came to me the other night, but I haven't had a chance to flesh it out. I thought we could do that now," he said, standing next to the bench and resting his hand on weathered planks near Wendy's shoulder.

"But we have that appointment," Wendy reminded him.

"Exactly. We could determine the timeline and the rules there, with a lawyer to moderate. Or mediate. Whatever it is that he does."

"She," Wendy corrected him. "And why, exactly, would I do this? After all these years, why would I want to put *more* time and energy into something I think is hopeless?"

Walter moved excitedly to sit next to her. "I'm glad you asked," he said, pulling a sheet of folded looseleaf from his pocket. "I researched just this morning. As of April—that's when these numbers were collected," he explained, "sixty percent of people who got divorced were happy they made that decision when asked six months later, but that number declined steadily over time. After a year, only fifty-five percent were happy; after three years, only thirty-eight percent were satisfied with their choice. After five years, eighteen percent and—here's the kicker—after ten years, *only five percent* of individuals were glad they'd gotten divorced."

Wendy stared at him, attempting to process this new information.

"People thought they wanted to get divorced," he continued, folding up the paper and slipping it back into his pocket, "but over time, they regretted it. That's why I think we should try. One last time, Wendy. We've been together so long, and we have children together—don't you think it's worth giving it another go? If only to make sure you want to do this?"

Wendy chewed on the inside of her cheek. He was a convincing bloke; she'd give him that.

"Fine," she said hesitantly, "but if I don't like the terms—"

"That's why we have the lawyer," Walter said jubilantly. Hopping off the bench, he began walking back toward the car. Wendy followed, shaking her head. After twenty-eight years, what was another month or two? And it wasn't the worst idea to be doubly sure before making a decision as monumental as this. Five percent? She took a deep breath and strode up the incline, stepping carefully to avoid getting dust on her leather flats.

Chapter Eight

"Welcome," Ms. Statterly said, holding her door open for Wendy and Walter to enter. Amazingly, they had arrived exactly on time despite their detour, and her office was on the main level making it easy to locate.

"I hope I didn't keep you waiting," she said, following behind them and slipping around her desk to take a seat.

"Not at all," Walter said, taking one of two available chairs in front of the desk. Wendy sat in the other, crossing her legs and folding her hands in her lap.

"So, what brings you in today?" she asked, her voice professional and her look polished. She pulled her tablet toward her and flipped it open.

"Well," Wendy started, "when I spoke with your secretary, I told her we wanted to meet with you to—" she paused, looking at Walter. "To determine next steps for a divorce."

"Yes," Ms. Statterly nodded, "that's what I've got written here, but what I need to know is: where you are in this process and what services are you looking for?"

Wendy took a deep breath. "Things have changed slightly since I made the appointment. We're still looking to get a divorce," she assured her hastily, "but we'd like to draft a sort-of...agreement. Or document—"

"A contract," Walter cut in, "that we would both abide by. To give one last shot at keeping our marriage," he said, looking pointedly at Wendy.

Ms. Statterly blinked in surprise. "You're looking to...save your marriage?"

"He is," Wendy muttered, pointing at Walter.

"I've done the research!" he said, defending himself.

"No need to justify," she said, focused intently on her screen, her fingers dancing on the wireless keyboard. "So...you'd like me to help you draft this contract?" she asked, pausing and looking up.

"For now," Wendy said. "We've never done anything like this."

"Neither have I," Ms. Statterly laughed, high and tinkling. "But I *am* very experienced with contracts in general. What exactly would you like it to say?"

"I thought we could throw out ideas—brainstorm—and then see where that takes us," Walter suggested.

"Sure," she agreed, reaching into her desk for a legal pad and pen. "Why don't you two throw out ideas, and I'll jot them down."

Wendy leaned back in her chair, turning slightly toward Walter.

"I'm thinking...six months—" he started.

"Too long," Wendy cut in.

"Alright...four?" he offered.

"Three."

"But that's not—"

"You want six, I want zero, so three seems perfectly reasonable," she said evenly.

Walter sighed, then nodded his acquiescence. "Three it is," he said. "And it has to be in Paris."

Wendy gasped in shock. "We've already discussed this, Walter. You wouldn't be able to—"

"Wendy, that's the one place you had on your list. Your dream location. There was only *one*," he emphasized, holding up a finger. "If we're going to give this thing a shot, I want it to be somewhere you're excited about. Neutral turf. I'll do what I need to figure out the business side of things, but please. Let me try."

She inspected his face, searching for any sign of the Walter —the old Walter—she'd been expecting in all this.

"I guess I can't say no to Paris," she said.

"I don't know who in their right mind would," Ms. Statterly commented, writing the word on the pad and circling it. "Three months in Paris, that's what we've got so far."

"Different flats," Wendy said, her eyes still locked on Walter. His skin flushed near his collar, but he didn't immediately jump in to counter.

"Is that okay with you, Walter?" Ms. Statterly asked, her pen poised over the parchment.

Walter nodded and then said softly, "Dates twice a week."

"Twice? Walter, we've never gone on that many dates per week in our whole lives—"

"I didn't argue about separate flats," he said, his voice hard. "If we're not living together, a few hours twice a week seems—how did you put it?—perfectly reasonable."

Wendy stared at him, folding her arms across her chest. "Who's going to plan them?" she asked.

"We'll split it. Fifty-fifty. One on Wednesday evening and one on Saturday."

"What if I'd like to go to a market on Saturday," Wendy shot back.

"The hours would be negotiable—with forty-eight hours notice—and you could even use a visit to the market *as* your date if you wanted."

Ms. Statterly scribbled furiously on her legal pad. Allowing her time to finish, Wendy waited before responding.

"Is that agreeable to both parties?" Ms. Statterly said finally, pointedly adding a period to her finished note.

Wendy nodded. "We're also allowed to go out with other...people," she added. This time, the flush on Walter's skin climbed past his collar and over his ears.

"You want to date people while we're still married?" he said, his voice heavy.

"No, Walt, I'm not saying 'date', I'm just saying that if I happen to get together with a group of female *and* male mates, I don't want you to lose your hair over it," Wendy explained.

Ms. Statterly looked between the two of them.

"Going out with your mates has never been a problem," Walter said, a slight edge in his tone that wasn't there previously.

"That's because I've never done it consistently," Wendy said under her breath.

"Okay then," Ms. Statterly said, ignoring the awkward comments and adding Wendy's point to the list. "Anything else? What about finances? That's usually what contracts are good for," she said with a laugh.

"We'll agree on the cost of our flats as we find good options—and whatever expenses go along with that—before signing a rental contract. Then we'll each get a budget of two hundred a month for groceries and—what do you think, Wendy? Seven hundred a month for other necessities and allowances?"

"That seems...fair," she answered, uncrossing her legs and shifting her weight on the chair. "I don't have much of an understanding of the cost of things there. Can we try those amounts for a month and then reconvene?"

Walter nodded.

Ms. Statterly looked at them appraisingly. "Not bad," she said, adding the amount to her notes. "Most couples take at least a few sessions to agree on a monthly stipend. Anything else we've missed?"

Wendy bit her lip nervously. "Walter," she said gently.

"Hmm?" he said, turning to face her.

"What happens when—if—we reach the end of the contract and...I'd still like a divorce?"

Walter cleared his throat. "Then...I'll sign whatever you need me to sign."

"No pushing? No trying to convince me that we should give it another go?" Wendy asked skeptically.

He shook his head. "You can put it in the contract if you like," he said, his face grim.

Ms. Statterly nodded, writing a single line at the bottom of her notes.

"Okay, if you'd like to wait just outside my office, I'll get this typed up, and we can look over it together and get your signatures to make it official."

Wendy nodded soberly, following Walter into the waiting room.

Chapter Nine

"Mum!" Calvin exclaimed, pulling an overnight bag from the boot of the car.

"You made it," Wendy smiled, stepping down onto the walkway with arms wide. For a moment, her heart squeezed as her mind flashed back to when he would run and hug her legs after school as a child, an expression of pure, boyish joy on his face.

"We did," Calvin said, walking up the driveway and wrapping his arms around his mother. Walter stepped out the front door onto the porch behind them just as Becky opened the passenger door and stepped onto the grass.

"Sorry," she said. "I had to send that last email. Now I'm free for the rest of the weekend."

Wendy greeted her with a warm embrace as Calvin moved past her to hug his father.

"Is Darrel able to make it, then?" Calvin asked.

"He'll be here after supper," Wendy said, ushering the group inside. "He agreed to let you two take the bedroom as long as he's allowed to tell Becky about 'Seven-Eleven the summer of 2012.' D'you have any idea what he's talking about?" Wendy asked with a laugh.

A guffaw burst out of Calvin, and he nearly dropped his bag on the stairs. "That story will never be told again, as far as I'm concerned."

"Well, you might have some negotiating to do, then," Wendy teased.

"You're going to let someone blackmail your favorite son? Under your very own roof?" Calvin said in mock disbelief.

Becky pushed him up the stairs rolling her eyes. "We'll get situated and be back in a minute," she said.

"Your mum's got dinner on the stove," Walter said, "so be quick about it."

"You can take your time," Wendy laughed. "He's just hungry."

She grinned as she walked into the kitchen and began to pull out dishes for setting the table.

"I can help with that," Walter said, picking up a stack of plates from the counter.

Wendy eyed him skeptically. "That's not in the contract," she said.

"It's not like I'm never helpful," Walter scoffed, turning and setting the plates on the table. "I'm usually home too late to join in with dinner preparation."

"No, Walter, I've always made dinner so it was ready for you when you got home," she explained, "which is why you're so hungry right now. You normally don't have to wait."

Walter pondered this a moment. "I've always enjoyed that," he admitted softly.

Wendy pursed her lips and turned to retrieve the cutlery.

Darrel arrived around eight o'clock as expected and quickly scarfed down a serving of shepherd's pie while the others were tidying up.

"How're your classes going?" Calvin asked, rinsing a dish and handing it to Wendy.

"Intense," Darrel admitted, "but doable. Definitely doable."

"Only a few weeks left," Becky said, scooping the last of the mashed potatoes into a Tupperware. "We lived for the end of the semester back in the day."

"You weren't taking summer classes," Darrel quipped.

"Don't you at least get a small break?" Calvin asked, and Darrel nodded.

"Two weeks," he said, bringing his plate to the counter. Walter took it from him, plunging it into the warm, soapy water in the sink.

"Will you be spending any of that time with us?" Wendy asked hopefully.

Darrel shook his head apologetically. "I'm going backpacking with a group that Tia hangs around with," he said.

"And Tia is?" Becky asked.

"A friend—we met in Calc. III."

"A 'friend,' eh?" Calvin teased, waggling his eyebrows at his brother.

"Sod off," Darrel said, punching Calvin's shoulder good-humouredly.

"Where're you going?" Walter asked, handing the last dish to Calvin and pulling the plug at the bottom of the sink.

"I'm not exactly sure," Darrel admitted. "I know we'll be spending some time in Zion and Bryce Canyon...beyond that," he shrugged. "They've got the whole itinerary planned; I'm sort of along for the ride."

"You have backpacking supplies?" Wendy asked.

"I bought a sleeping bag and pad, but I'm going to sleep in a tent with one of the others."

"Tia?" Calvin said provocatively.

"No, Cal, we're just friends," Darrel laughed with a hint of annoyance.

"Well, I think it sounds lovely," Wendy said, turning and drying her hands on the dish towel hanging from the stove handle. Taking a nervous breath, she steeled herself and turned toward them. "Your dad and I are actually heading out on our own adventure this summer."

Calvin, Becky, and Darrel stopped what they were doing and fixed their eyes on hers. Walter cleared his throat.

"We've decided to take a holiday. To Paris," Walter said.

"To Paris?" Calvin repeated, his eyes wide. "When?"

"We're not quite sure, exactly. Hopefully, we'll be able to leave in a month or so. There're a lot of loose ends to tie up at the office, and I need to find a lawn company—"

"A landscaping company? How long will you be going?" Darrel questioned.

Wendy looked down, fiddling with the ties on her apron.

"Three months," Walter announced confidently.

"Three months!?" Calvin and Becky said in unison.

"You two haven't taken a holiday in at least ten years, and now, all of a sudden, you're leaving the country for three months?" Darrel asked, shock evident in his face.

"It's about time, don't you think?" Walter said jovially. "We've worked hard, raised the both of you, paid our dues—"

"But Dad, you *hate* traveling," Calvin cut in. Wendy couldn't help but feel validated with this comment, though she didn't want to show it. She quickly took to wiping the cabinet doors under the sink.

"Remember that time we went to Steamboat?" Calvin continued. "We were supposed to stay for a week, but you made us come home after four days because you were too anxious being away from home that long."

"I wasn't anxious," Walter argued.

"That was the longest trip we ever took!" Calvin continued. "You think you'll be able to handle months in a new place? With no predictable routine or familiarity?"

Walter smoothed his moustache. "Is it a crime to want to do something different?"

"Was this your idea?" Darrel asked, looking to his mother.

"We decided on this together," she shrugged, rinsing her cloth and draping it over the faucet.

After a long pause, Calvin ran his hands through his dark hair. "Well," he sighed, glancing at Becky. "Since we're all making big announcements here...Mum, Dad. Becky and I...we're expecting."

Wendy's hand flew to her mouth. "Oh!" she exclaimed. "That's—that's—"

"Wonderful news," Walter congratulated, pulling his son into an embrace and clapping him on the back. Wendy rushed to Becky and wrapped her arms around her.

"I'm absolutely speechless," she said, stepping back to wipe the tears from her eyes. "How far along are you?" she asked, looking at Becky's midsection in awe.

"About twelve weeks," she said.

"So exciting," Wendy said under her breath.

"You can have fun on your trip," Calvin said, "but we need you back here by the end of September, alright?" he teased.

"I wouldn't miss it," Wendy laughed, scurrying down the hall to find a tissue.

"That makes my backpacking announcement fairly underwhelming, doesn't it?" Darrel muttered good-humoredly. "Thanks for one-upping me as usual, Cal."

Calvin reached over and pulled him into a headlock.

"We'll all be thrilled to hear about how things went with Tia," he said obnoxiously as Darrel wrestled free of his grip.

After smoothing his hair, Darrel grinned. "I'm happy for you two," he said. "Truly."

Calvin pulled Becky close and put an arm around her shoulder.

"We wanted to try sooner," Becky admitted as Wendy walked back into the room, "but Calvin didn't feel comfortable starting a family before his last year of residency."

"Understandable," Walter said. "Very practical."

Wendy shot him a knowing look. "Let's have dessert, shall we?" she said, pushing through the group to get to the stove. "I made your favorite. Sticky toffee pudding," she announced proudly.

Sighs of gratitude echoed behind her, and her heart was full to bursting as she pulled the steaming ceramic dish from the oven.

Chapter Ten

MAY, 2014

"And this," Walter demonstrated, "is the alarm system. I've included the code in the binder, but I thought I'd show you where the buttons are."

"Sure," Tia nods. "I can't promise I'm going to keep it set every night...is that okay?"

"Whatever you feel comfortable with, dear," Wendy said. "We've put our valuables in storage, and if someone wants to steal our furniture, all the better for us," she laughed.

"Are you going to bring anything back from Paris?" Tia asked, paying only partial attention to Walter's finger motions.

"I doubt it," Wendy muttered.

"And then you hit this button here to deactivate it," Walter said, pressing the bottom button and closing the console.

"Got it," Tia said. "Thanks again for letting me stay here for the summer.

"You're doing us the favour," Wendy said warmly. "This

was the part I was most nervous about—making sure the house was taken care of."

"Well, it was a win-win," Tia said. "When Darrel mentioned you'd be leaving it empty and I was looking for a short-term lease, it seemed too good to be true."

"Should I be offended that Darrel will most likely visit twice as often while we're gone?" Walter teased, walking up the stairs to retrieve their luggage.

"He's already neck-deep in Environmental Systems, so I highly doubt that," Tia laughed.

Walter trundled down the stairs a few moments later with a large suitcase, placed it in the living room, and turned for another trip. Wendy pulled it to the entry, holding the screen door open with her left leg as she hoisted the bag over the sill to the porch. Turning, she found two smaller roller bags now waiting in the room and followed the same procedure.

Eventually, Wendy and Walter stood side-by-side on the porch with their bags, leaving Tia alone in their house. Scanning over their limited belongings, Wendy suddenly felt a pang of anxiety rise in her chest. She hadn't ever gone back to Europe without a firm plan that almost always included staying with friends or family. Now, they were 'catching an Uber' with a random stranger, hopping on a plane, taking another presumably dangerous form of transportation to separate flats in Paris where she'd be meeting *on her own* with yet another stranger. There would likely be a language barrier nearly everywhere she went, and then there was the fact that she'd be sleeping alone. Her head began to throb, and as the white sedan pulled up to the curb, she gripped her luggage with shaking hands.

"License plate matches," Walter said, craning his neck to see the back of the car and comparing it to the screen of the smartphone Calvin had insisted he purchase before traveling.

"Let's go then," Wendy said, marching down the steps

with bags in hand, attempting to conceal her momentary mental breakdown. She focused on the task at hand to prevent her mind from spinning out of control into a full-blown panic attack. Once seated in the backseat, she looked behind her at the house through the window and held her breath as the car moved slowly away from the curb.

"We've begun our descent..." the pilot said through the overhead speaker, startling Wendy out of a fitful sleep. She'd taken approximately seven naps on the flight, none of which lasted more than fifteen or twenty minutes. Her legs ached, and she felt desperate to stand and walk around. Now, with that announcement, she'd missed her chance to at least stroll to the back of the plane to use the loo.

She yawned, stretching her arms above her head.

"Good flight?" Walter asked next to her.

Wendy shrugged. "As good as could be expected," she said.

"Mine too," he said. "I'd venture we have about thirty minutes left before we land." Walter paused, opening the window shade to take a look at the landscape, but the cloud cover was too thick to see the city below.

"Would you like me to help you get to your flat?" Walter asked.

"It's early afternoon; I think it'll be fine. Nobody murders someone in their cab in the middle of the day," she said dryly.

"There's always a first," Walter retorted, and she rolled her eyes. "We're only ten blocks from each other, so don't hesitate—"

"I'll be fine, Walt," she said, reaching into her handbag for her lemon lip balm.

"I know," he said softly, fiddling with his tray table. "But we *are* only ten blocks away," he repeated slowly. "Would it be alright if I at least called tonight to make sure you made it safely?"

"That'd be fine," Wendy agreed, "though I'll probably sack out once I get unpacked."

Walter chuckled. "I'll call early, then," he said.

"Maybe tomorrow I should practice texting so I can let the boys know we made it," Wendy laughed.

"You can send your practice notes to me. I'm horribly slow," Walter lamented. "With these sausage fingers, how can I possibly hit the correct button even fifty percent of the time?"

Wendy laughed out loud. "You need a sausage-finger-sized phone," she teased.

"It sounds worse when you say it," Walter said, inspecting his hands.

The flight attendants walked down the aisles checking for seatbelts and proper positioning of chairs and tray tables. The clouds finally dissipated to a fine mist outside of Walter's window, and Wendy craned her neck to get a glimpse of the buildings below.

"Can you spot any landmarks?" she asked.

"I see a few interesting spots, but I'm not sure what they are," Walter admitted. "Like there," he said pointing.

"Mmm," Wendy said, following his finger to a large dome protruding from a hillside. "I'm not sure either. It'll be fun to explore, won't it?" she said excitedly.

Walter remained silent next to her, but Wendy didn't notice his hesitation. She was dazzled by the newness that lay before her. Only hours ago, she was nearly paralyzed by the unknown, but now—beholding the beauty of it—she felt nothing but pure positive energy.

Sitting up straight, she busied herself with organizing her bags, making sure she had everything she'd taken out during the flight.

“So I guess—after we find our bags—the next time I’ll see you will be Wednesday,” Walter said, almost to himself.

“That’s right,” Wendy said off-handedly, nearly breathless with anticipation of her new adventure.

“My turn to plan the first one?” he asked.

“If you don’t mind,” she said quickly, bracing her arms against the seat for landing.

As the plane hit the runway, she closed her eyes until the momentum forcing her back into her seat lifted. When the aircraft came to a stop, she quickly unbuckled and stood in the aisle to pull her carry-on bag from the hatch. Wendy waited patiently while the passengers in front of her collected their things and slowly walked off the plane. When the row in front of them emptied, Wendy quickly followed the line of people, her back to Walter as he stood to pull his bag to the floor.

Walter caught up to her about half-way through the airport. He was short of breath when he attempted to casually take the space next to her. They were nearly at the baggage claim before she noticed his presence.

“I thought you stopped somewhere back there,” she said.

“Convenient that we’re all going to the same place,” he said confidently, ironically attempting to hide his quick pace and obvious lack of physical fitness—from the one person who had seen him every day for half his life.

They rounded the corner, found their carousel, and then scouted out a place to stand and watch for their bags. Faster than Walter would have liked, the turnstile engaged, and bags began flowing onto the belt.

“Ah!” Wendy exclaimed, setting her things next to Walter and walking to pull her bag from the train of luggage. He wasn’t even aware of his bag’s arrival because he couldn’t take his eyes off her. Arriving at their mutual waiting spot with her checked bag, Wendy quickly attached her carry-on, slipped on her jacket, slung her handbag over her shoulder, and pulled out her phone.

"First time using this Uber app," she said. "Wish me luck?"

"Good luck, Wendy," Walter said sincerely as he watched her turn on her heel and disappear through the sliding glass doors.

Chapter Eleven

JUNE, 1985

Walter Winslow led Wendy Presbury—his girlfriend of exactly four-and-a-half years—under the archway announcing the entrance to Avondale Park. He couldn't have planned this day more perfectly. The sun was shining for the first time in nearly two weeks and the park was surprisingly—blissfully—quiet for a Friday evening.

Walter had AAT qualification the week before and Wendy had been badgering him incessantly to do something to celebrate. To him, spending two years studying engineering only to realize the path he'd mapped out wasn't leading where he'd hoped felt like nothing at all to be celebrated. Sure, he'd eventually settled on accounting, but he'd wasted years of his time and—more importantly—put their progress together on hold. He didn't know how to express that the only thing he actually felt like celebrating was the ring he'd finally purchased two weeks before.

Pretending to give in to Wendy's request, but with plans of his own, he'd agreed to go with her to the park for a celebratory picnic. Now—with one hand lugging the wicker picnic basket—she was quite literally pulling him along the path to the lake with child-like enthusiasm.

"What's the hurry?" Walter laughed, trying to keep up.

"I'm so excited, I can't help it!" Wendy said, her breath coming in bursts.

"Excited for what?" Walter asked. "We've got all night, I don't understand—"

But then he saw it. A huge sign that said "Congratulations Walter" on it, being held by his best mates along with his sister, Lucy, and their friend Mary.

"How—what is this?" Walter asked in shock. "I thought we were having a small picnic—"

"Surprise!" Wendy laughed giddily as the group motioned to their own picnic baskets sitting on the lawn.

Walter felt his face flush, but began walking slowly as Wendy beckoned him forward. He wasn't prepared for a large group gathering. He had mapped this evening out in his head, and it took him a moment to shift gears. Plastering a smile on his face, he approached his mates. As they embraced him and clapped him on the back, he absorbed some of their light-hearted energy and felt slightly more at ease.

His heart was still hammering in his chest as the banner was rolled up and picnic blankets were spread out on the green grass. Walter stood on the grassy knoll and gazed at the lake, wishing he could relax and enjoy the glistening water and the trees softly swaying in the breeze, but he couldn't. Not fully. It was as if a barrier stood between him and gaeity—a mound of expectations he'd created and yet couldn't comprehend how to sweep away.

He turned back in frustration and walked toward Wendy who was beckoning for him to join her on the blanket. Opening her basket, she pulled out a tantalizing spread: scotch eggs, crisps, cucumber salad, and two pieces of his favorite tomato quiche. The food was almost enough to make him forget about what he held in his pocket and the dashed plans that surrounded it.

Realizing he wouldn't be able to eat at all in his current state, he searched for another path for the evening. If he thought his anxiety over this moment was bad before, having a crowd present made it exponentially worse, but he steeled himself. He could do this. Sure, it wouldn't be what he'd initially envisioned, but Wendy wouldn't know the difference. Wiping a bead of sweat from his forehead, he closed his hand around the small box and spun toward the group before he could lose courage.

"Everyone, I have something I need to say before we pull out our supper," he announced. Friendly faces turned toward him, and he swallowed hard. "Wendy," he said, reaching for her hand and pulling her off the blanket to stand next to him. "Thank you for planning such a lovely surprise, but I have to be honest. While it's lovely to see each and every one of you," he said, speaking to everyone, "I was looking forward to spending the evening alone. With you," he finished, looking intently into her eyes.

His mates whistled, and Walter grinned, feigning confidence.

"Because," he continued, "I can't wait one more moment to ask you this."

Walter dropped to one knee and pulled his hand from his pocket, opening his fingers to reveal the velvet ring box he'd been carrying with him every day since he's purchased it.

Wendy gasped in shock, her hands flying to her mouth.

"Wendy Presbury. I haven't been able to keep you off my mind since that day at the pub, and that's saying something because I've been writing endless exams in two different areas of study for the last few years. And I really love numbers," he laughed nervously, his hands shaking. "I don't know what my future will look like, but I'm positive I want you in it. Wendy, will you marry me?" Walter finished, the blood rushing so loudly in his ears that he gave himself a sixty-five percent chance of passing out.

Tears streamed down Wendy's cheeks as she nodded her head emphatically up and down, lowering her hand. Cheers rang out around them as Walter slipped the ring on her finger and stood, lifting her into his arms.

Chapter Twelve

MAY, 2014

The magnitude of his life choices settled fully onto Walter as he made his way toward a five-story apartment complex. The wheels of his roller bag clicked violently against the cobblestones of the street, as they had done for the last four blocks. After waiting fifteen minutes in front of what looked like an entrance to a public house, he'd finally broken down and called the number on the rental agreement. This led him to discover he'd been pronouncing the street name incorrectly and was loitering in front of the wrong building altogether.

"Bonjour," a woman with sleek black hair and red lips greeted him as he finally approached the correct address. "Walter?" she asked, with only a hint of a French accent.

"Oui," Walter said, nodding.

"Your keys," she said, handing him an envelope. "Up the stairs, third floor, number 302. This code—3447—opens the gate. The large key opens the complex," she said, motioning to the arched, wooden doors beyond the wrought iron bars before them, "and the smaller key opens your door."

Walter stared at the envelope, then at the formidable building in front of him. "Thank you, merci," he said, moving his bags to the side and pulling out the larger key.

"If you need anything, you 'ave my email, yes?" she asked.

Again, Walter nodded.

"Good," she said with a smile, turning briskly. "Au revoir."

Walter gave a small wave as she retreated down the cobbled walkway. He entered the code, heard a slight click, and quickly pushed. The gate swung open with a creak, and Walter held it open with his knee, awkwardly rolling his bags into the small courtyard. Once through, he allowed the gate to swing shut with a clang. Taking a deep breath, he lifted his luggage and began the arduous climb up the narrow stairway.

After ascending exactly eleven stairs and pausing on the first-floor landing, Walter leaned against the wall to catch his breath. Leaving his roller bag forlornly in the hall, he walked the remaining stairs carrying only his jacket, shoulder bag, and carry-on. Setting them by the door, he then retraced his steps, wiping the sweat from his forehead as he descended the stairs to retrieve his suitcase.

Finally, at the door of his new, temporary home, he inspected the elegant brass knob and the birds that seemed to dance along the burgundy frame. He admired the detail and intricate handiwork as he caught his breath, but all love and admiration died in his heart when he inserted the key and could not, for the life of him, get it to turn. Not even a smidgen. He tried left, then right. He pulled it out a few millimeters and attempted to turn it again in this position with no luck.

"Go on, now," he urged, willing the key to magically twist and put him out of his misery. Finally, placing his hand on the knob and turning it in frustration, the key clicked slightly to the side. Once the mechanism was in the correct position, the lock turned surprisingly easily, given its ancient appearance.

"Ha!" he blurted, turning the knob fully and opening the door. Jubilantly, he pulled his luggage inside, closed the door behind him, and collapsed on the single upholstered chair in the cramped sitting room.

Wendy waited patiently in the stationary vehicle's passenger seat, listening to her Uber driver prattle on about American politics in broken English. She nodded graciously, smiling, and murmuring the occasional 'Mmmhmm.' When she noticed a break in his diatribe, she quickly opened her door.

"Thank you," she said hastily, stepping to the street. "I appreciate the ride." She had already settled up on the app, leaving what she thought was a generous tip, considering the one-sided conversation she'd endured for the last thirty minutes. Pulling her bags from the backseat, she waved as the young man drove off.

Turning, she pulled her bags to the large French doors of her building. The manager was supposed to be meeting her, but it seemed that he was late. Wendy scanned the street, and —upon finding it empty—she sat down on top of her roller bag to give her legs a break. Up the road, she noticed a boulangerie and wished she didn't have her luggage so she could peruse the shop. Though, at this time of day, she wasn't sure what would be left in the way of bread or pastries. She'd have to stop by first thing in the morning. The idea thrilled her—waking early to explore around her building in the 5th Arrondissement, then the rest of the Latin Quarter and beyond. Three months had seemed like a long time until she began making a list of everything she wanted to see.

"Pardon madame?" a voice startled her.

"Oh," she said, quickly rising to her feet. "Yes, are you Louis?" she asked, her eyes wandering over the man's wavy salt and pepper hair, his five o'clock shadow, and v-neck cotton shirt with the sleeves rolled casually to his elbows.

"Oui, bonjour," he said, flashing a charming smile.

She suddenly felt shaky and found herself smoothing her hair and clearing her throat.

"Your keys," he said, handing her a metal ring. "Second floor," he pointed upward. "212," he said, miming the numbers with his fingers. Motioning for the keys, he gestured to a large, brass key dangling from the metal band.

"Like this," he said, inserting it into the slot next to her.

"Ah," she said. "And this one is for my apartment?"

"Oui," he answered, nodding gratefully.

"Thank you," she said.

"Le carnet—ummm," he hesitated, "notebook?" he questioned, and Wendy nodded, encouraging him. "Notebook—dans la cuisine..."

"Kitchen?" Wendy guessed hopefully.

"Oui! Kitchen," he repeated. "Les directives—pour...garbage, lights—" he stammered.

"Yes!" Wendy exclaimed. "Instructions. For the apartment."

"Oui, c'est bon," he said, shoving his hands in his back pockets.

"Thank you, Louis," she said again. "I'll call if I have any questions."

He nodded, flashing her another smile before walking down the street. Taking a deep breath, Wendy hoisted her bags through the doors to the landing. Noticing an elevator to the right, she pressed the button, then waited for it to announce its arrival. When it dinged, she pulled the outer doors open and—upon stepping into the elevator and attempting to bring the bags in with her—quickly realized there wasn't room on the floor for all of them.

Thinking quickly, she stepped back onto the tile floor,

pushed her bags into the elevator, pressed the second floor, and then promptly closed the outer doors and hustled up the stairs. She made it to the doors in plenty of time and removed her bags from the cage as soon as the doors opened. Pulling them down the hall, she soon found her door, opened it with the key Louis had given her, and walked inside.

After spending the evening inspecting every inch of the place, Wendy emptied her clothes into the wardrobe in the bedroom and quickly stripped down for a shower. Entering the cramped space, she pulled the curtain around her *and* the toilet and turned on the warm water. Choosing to ignore the bare wiring along the ceiling above her, she closed her eyes and scrubbed her body, rinsing away the grime that had accumulated over nearly twenty-four hours of travel. The cascade of water over her head felt heavenly, even though she had to lean down to catch the spray.

After drying off and dressing in her pajamas, she pulled digestive biscuits and an apple from her travel bag. Tomorrow she'd go to the market, but this would have to do for tonight. She took her makeshift dinner to the couch and flopped down, resting her feet on the small coffee table in front of her. Sighing, she bit into the apple, glanced at the art on the walls around her, and smiled contentedly.

Chapter Thirteen

Wendy woke the next morning with a terrible headache. Stumbling out of bed, she made her way to the bathroom and rifled through her toiletries bag until she found the small bottle of Excedrin she'd thrown into her things at the last minute. Popping one into her mouth, she leaned over the sink and took a drink directly from the tap. Then, pulling her shoulder-length hair back with an elastic, she allowed cold water from the tap to pool in her hands, then splashed it onto her face.

With her head still pounding, she returned to her bed—behind a small partition in the main living space of the studio apartment—and tidied it. She pulled her suitcase in front of the wardrobe next to the bed and flipped it onto its side. Tugging on the zipper, she opened it and began to pull out her belongings.

She carefully organized her clothes on the shelves, then pushed her empty luggage under the bed. Throwing on a loose skirt and blouse, she returned to the bathroom to put on her makeup. Her stomach growled as she dabbed concealer over the dark circles beneath her eyes. Not even bothering to put on mascara, she swiped a bit of color over her lips and pulled her hair up into a clip, then slipped on her flats and double-checked that her new keys were in her purse before walking out the door.

Making it to the street, she couldn't help but gape at the stylishly dressed men and women striding along the walkways with purpose. She determined instantly to visit a shop and purchase a few more suitable items of clothing. Searching the shops from her position in front of her building, she spotted the boulangerie she'd noticed the evening before. Heading that direction, she pulled out her phone and began searching for a supermarket.

When Walter opened his eyes, his chest immediately seized, and his heart began palpitating. Whipping his head from side to side as he sat upright in bed, realization began to dawn, and his death grip on the comforter loosened slightly. He thankfully remembered why he was in this foreign apartment, but that didn't immediately assuage his anxiety. What had he been thinking? Coming to this new place where he knew no one and had minimal experience with the culture. What was he going to *do* for three months?

Rubbing his eyes, he checked the clock and saw that it was already seven-thirty. Though, what did that actually mean? He hadn't the foggiest what time it was in Colorado, and his body was so turned around it didn't matter. He lowered his feet to the floor and carefully descended the seven steps of the loft ladder to land in the joint kitchen and living area.

Opening the fridge, he pulled out the yoghurt he'd purchased at the market a few doors down. After taking a small nap the evening before, he'd decided to pick up a few necessities before turning in for the night, and this morning he couldn't have been more grateful.

With his blood sugar at an appropriate level, the thought of wandering around foreign streets sounded intriguing instead of panic-inducing. After all, he had to find some way of filling his time—at least for the next day and a half until Wednesday. Pulling out his tablet—which he'd used only a handful of times back home—he followed the instructions from the sheet on the counter to connect it to WiFi. He pulled up Google maps and began scanning the area. He quickly put a pin in Wendy's location, then zoomed out to see a ten-block radius surrounding their flats.

Notre Dame seemed like the obvious choice for their first date, but in the back of his brain he remembered hearing somewhere—was it Ted at the office?— that reservations were recommended. Typing the famous church into the search bar, he scrolled and found a calendar. As he suspected, this Wednesday was not going to be a viable option unless they wanted to risk standing in line. And *the* famous cathedral in Paris in the summer would definitely merit long lines regardless of the time of day.

Back to the maps, he decided that it might be a decent idea to stroll along the Seine and pick up dinner on the way. Everything within him screamed to do something bigger—more flashy and awe-inspiring—but they had three months. If he came out with something ostentatious now, how would he top that later?

With his mind made up, he turned off his screen, rummaged through his carry-on for a charger and adapter, and plugged the tablet into the singular outlet on the kitchen wall. Placing his phone, wallet, and keys in his pocket, he bravely strode to the front door, opened it, and stepped outside.

Chapter Fourteen

Wendy Winslow felt like a million pounds by the time she returned to her flat. She carried at least eight bags in her arms, some of which held groceries and freshly baked bread and pastries. She hungrily unpacked her loot at the kitchen counter, setting the bags that had non-food items next to her bed.

As much as she had wanted to walk into every boutique she passed, she decided that buying any sort of clothing needed to wait for a couple of weeks. She pulled fresh vegetables—rapini, fennel, carrots, peppers, and tomatoes—from her paper sacks and placed them in the fridge with excitement. Wendy was resolutely determined to set exercise goals, and she was *going* to lose weight. Or at least a few sizes, whichever came first. And if the French did it by eating fresh vegetables *and* bread, who was she to do differently?

Immediately after closing the refrigerator door, she reached into her carry on and pulled out her notepad and pen. 'Paris Goals' she wrote across the top of the sheet in loopy letters, then quickly scribbled over the word 'goals' and wrote 'dreams' instead. She divided the paper into two columns. On one side, she wrote 'what' and on the other, she wrote 'how.' Then she began listing her items in bullet points. 'Lose Weight' was the first on the list, and under the 'how' section, she wrote: I will walk ten miles around Paris each day. I will learn how to do push-ups and sit-ups in my flat. I will eat fresh everything, mostly vegetables.

She lifted her hand to admire her handiwork. Merely looking at it on paper felt exhilarating. And terrifying. But wasn't this the perfect opportunity to make these changes? A new place with none of the old habits and routines to get in the way? She looked again at the words 'lose weight' and scribbled them out. 'Feel strong and vibrant' she wrote above it, then smiled to herself. She'd still wait a few weeks to buy clothes.

Reaching the bottom of the sheet, she assessed the 'how' section. 'Try something new every day,' 'meditate for ten minutes morning and night,' 'complete one french lesson each weekday (you can take weekends off).' Her heart was nearly bursting in anticipation of the new life she was creating, but her body was exhausted from hauling bags for miles around the city. 'Take a power nap as needed,' she wrote hastily in the margin, then set down the pen and walked to her bed.

When her alarm sounded fifteen minutes later, she stretched her arms above her head and took a cleansing breath. Flicking off the blanket, she stood and adjusted her shirt. It was nearly dusk, judging by the light filtering in through the window. Tonight she was going to explore the Paris nightlife and there wasn't a second to lose.

Pulling a simple black wrap dress from the wardrobe, she hurriedly dressed and coiffed her hair, then put a little rouge on her cheeks and applied mascara. Though she still looked tired from the time change, she figured there wasn't a quick fix for that, and grabbed her purse as she walked out the door.

From her earlier adventures, she gathered that Rue Mouffetard would be a solid bet for good food and possibly live music. The signs she had passed earlier in the afternoon advertised as much, so she headed that direction. Sure enough, as she reached the intersection, she could hear forks clinking on plates, people engaged in lively conversation, and music filling the air.

Energy buzzed around her as she turned and walked up the narrow road. She stopped at each restaurant, looking over their menu and prices. Finally, she stopped at La Crète and nodded when the host asked her if she'd like a seat in the front window. She decided on a Greek salad and lamb chops before setting her menu down and watching—with interest—the people strolling along the street outside her window.

People walked through the restaurant door a few at a time until conversation filled the dining room, and Wendy felt a part of something. A participant in Paris, if that's a thing. As requested, a bottle of Perrier arrived at her table, and she quickly poured a glass and took a sip.

Outside the window, one couple in particular caught her eye. Both quite fashionable, their hands were entwined, and they kissed each other no less than four times in the brief moments she had been watching. She began to write a narrative in her mind of the passionate love affair preceding their daring elopement to Paris when suddenly, she caught her breath.

There—across the street, window shopping alone—was Walter. He looked exactly as he had the day before, but somehow, seeing him in this context—especially out and about *on his own*—sent Wendy for a loop. What was he doing? Why was he looking in the shop windows? Was he looking for something to purchase, or was it simple curiosity?

When he hesitated in front of the sign for Bistrot 88, Wendy had the acute desire to stand, walk to the door, and warn him that he'd probably like the food at La Crète much better. Forcing herself to unclench her fingers from the edge of the table, she took a deep breath. She watched Walter enter the bistrot and the door swing shut.

"Madame?" the waiter said, clearing his throat.

"Oh, yes, I'm sorry," she said. "I'd like the salad to start, and then I'll have the lamb chops," she instructed, pointing at the menu in case he didn't speak English well. Though she had been gaining more confidence in her French, she wasn't going to waste a perfectly good opportunity to speak English and *not* feel stressed by the interaction.

"Oui, c'est bon," he said, taking the menu from her and retreating with a nod.

Wendy turned again to the window, but this time she noticed a young girl—likely mid-twenties—with a long, dark ponytail and glasses inspecting the menu in front of her. The girl's eyebrow furrowed, and she pulled out her phone and typed something in. She looked back at the menu, nodded, then approached the door.

Looking around the small dining room, Wendy recognized immediately that there wasn't an open table for the woman. Though she knew there were plenty of restaurants along this particular street, the girl looked so disappointed when the host explained that she'd be looking at a forty-five-minute wait at a minimum that Wendy stood and approached the pair.

"Excusez moi," she said gently. "Would you like to sit at my table?" she offered, and the girl's face lit up.

"You speak English?" she said excitedly in an American accent.

Wendy laughed. "I do," she said. "Would you like to join me?"

"Yes," she said gratefully, thanking the host as she followed Wendy to her table a few paces away.

"Where're you from?" the girl asked, slinging her purse across the back of the chair.

"Originally? From England, but most recently? Colorado."

"No way!" she exclaimed. "I'm from California."

"I could've guessed that," Wendy commented under her breath, bringing her glass to her lips.

Seemingly none the wiser, the girl continued. "I'm studying at the Paris Sciences et Lettres. Well, I mean, I will be in the fall. I arrived a few weeks early to get settled."

"Are you feeling settled?" Wendy asked.

"This is day four," she said, "so....no?"

Just then, the waiter approached and the girl gave her order—souvlaki and the hummus plate. When he left the table, she turned again to Wendy.

"I didn't catch your name," Wendy said.

"Cami," she answered. "What's yours?"

"I'm Wendy. What are you studying at—at that school?" she asked, the name escaping her.

"It's a masters degree, called the 'Ecole Normale Superieure.' I want to teach humanities and this program was a fraction of the cost of programs in the US."

"It's taught in French?"

"Both, a mix of English and French. It's not that my French is terrible, it's just that it's exhausting thinking in a second language. After a few days, I'm ready for a break."

"Good practice for when class starts," Wendy commented, and the girl hesitantly acknowledged the truth of the statement.

Their waiter approached the table, setting Wendy's salad and Cami's hummus plate in front of them.

"I'm starving," Cami said, grabbing a pita chip from the plate.

Wendy took a bite of her salad, enjoying the crisp lettuce and tangy vinaigrette. "Do you know anyone here?" she asked, swallowing.

"I've met my roommate digitally—we live a few streets over, closer to the school—but she hasn't arrived yet. Other than that...I know you," she said laughing.

"Well I don't know anyone either," Wendy admitted.

"Wait, you're new here, too?" Cami asked between bites.

"I arrived yesterday."

Cami's eyes widened. "Vacation?"

"Of sorts," Wendy nodded. "I'm here for three months."

"Sounds amazing," Cami said. Wiping her hands with her napkin, she reached around the back of her chair. "Here's what I think we should do," she said, pulling her phone from her purse. "Nobody likes eating dinner alone, right? Would you like to meet up a few times a week? We could text and choose a spot? Try out a few restaurants?"

"I'd love to," Wendy said, mentally checking off three distinct items on her Paris Dreams list for the day. She smiled to herself as she daintily scooped the last bit of olive and feta from her bowl.

Chapter Fifteen

Walter's meal at Bistrot 88 was just...okay. Nothing to write home about, but not terrible either, just disappointing. He'd made the classic mistake of ordering the burger—American style—thinking the barbeque sauce and cheddar would be exactly what he was used to and serve as a comfort to him. It wasn't and it didn't. If anything, it only succeeded in reiterating to him how different his life was at this point and how much he missed his predictable routine at home. It felt like years since he'd watched Xena, and he was still vaguely curious about whether her baby survived Athena's wrath or not...

Looking up, he was surprised to see he'd already made it home. A deep sense of loneliness enveloped him as he passed through the gate and toward the stairs to his flat. Today had been enjoyable enough. He'd purchased groceries, window shopped, and scouted out a possible route for his date with Wendy tomorrow evening. He'd enjoyed the architecture and the weather was immensely pleasant. But somehow, walking up to an empty flat felt—well, it felt a little pathetic.

As he placed his key in the lock with the handle twisted just so, he opened the door and flicked on the light. Turning the deadbolt securely, he walked into the kitchen for a glass of water. It was only eight o'clock and, though he could go to sleep early—his body certainly needed the extra rest—he didn't quite feel like crawling into bed yet. Instead, he set his glass on the counter and walked the few steps to the sitting area, opening the small cupboard doors on the stand underneath the telly.

To his delight, he found nine DVD's and curiously inspected each one. They were, of course, all French, which meant he'd never heard of them. Three of them listed English subtitles as an option thankfully, so he randomly chose one and popped it in the player. 'Amour' was the title, and an older couple was displayed on the cover. He wasn't convinced it was his sort of movie, but with indefinite time on his hands, what did he have to lose?

Two and a half hours later, Walter sat weeping in the chair as he watched the credits, using the palm of his hand to wipe away tears that freely leaked over his cheeks. He knew she was going to die. The opening scene made that clear, so why was he sobbing like a ten-year-old boy? Georges had been so...loyal. Such a loving companion. Walter sighed heavily as he stood, walking to the bathroom to splash his face with water.

He inspected himself in the mirror. His blue eyes stared back at him, haunted and desperate. He didn't want to be alone for the rest of his life, and he didn't want to find someone new. He wanted Wendy, but she didn't believe that he could be the man *she* wanted. The man she needed. Truth be told, he didn't either. Walter couldn't have described that man in detail if his life depended on it, but somehow he needed to prove to her that he was him. The man of her dreams. But where to start?

His eyes landed on the swath of hair growing above his

upper lip. He'd had a moustache since the third year of their marriage. The style was in at the time, and he'd never considered that it may have gone out a long time ago. Clenching his jaw, he searched his toiletry bag for his razor. Plugging it in, he took a deep breath and then turned it on.

The next morning—with an unusually cold upper lip—Walter Winslow left the apartment and walked to the café on the corner. Tonight was his date with Wendy and that felt worthy of a celebration.

Sitting at a table outside under the canopy, he sipped his deliciously thick hot cocoa and anticipated his tartine. Though he'd only had it once, the soft french bread smothered with butter and jam had quickly become his new favorite thing. It wasn't the healthiest of breakfasts, but considering he'd walked nearly twenty miles over the last two days, he figured he'd give himself a break. When his plate arrived, he savored each bite, enjoying the satisfying crunch of the crust and how the butter melted on his tongue.

After settling the check, he began his jaunt toward the starting point of an audio tour he'd researched before arriving in France. There were over fifteen different tours he'd been interested in and today he was beginning with the shortest one. Since he'd be walking this evening as well, he didn't want to tire himself out prematurely.

Walter arrived at the starting point for the tour: Place St. Michel. Setting his headphones over his ears, he pressed play and slipped his phone into his pocket. He followed the instructions exactly, moving from place to place without needing to pause, and thoroughly enjoyed the ancient stories, notes on architecture, and historical highlights as he walked. As he passed other tourists with their headphones on, he smiled inwardly at the small thrill it gave him to be experiencing a place alone, but yet communally at the exact same time. He found himself marveling at the diversity around him —the myriad languages and observable differences in culture.

When he reached the end of the last track, his mind was exploding with thoughts he hadn't entertained in...probably ever. A little shop sat on the corner selling knick-knacks, and his eyes were drawn to a stack of journals. His heart leaped, and he speed-walked back to his apartment, took the stairs two at a time—stopping on the landing to catch his breath—and burst into his apartment to retrieve the notebook he'd stashed off-handedly in his luggage. Plucking it from his bag along with a pen, he left his apartment—completely forgetting to lock the door behind him—and descended to the street.

After heading north for a few blocks, he found a bench under the shade of a beautiful tree next to the bridge leading across the Seine to the Notre Dame Cathedral. He sat there, content, gazing at the beauty of the river and art vendors, absorbing the hustle and bustle of the city around him. Then he opened his journal to the first page and began to write.

Chapter Sixteen

Wendy was late. They had agreed to meet at the south corner of Square Viviani at precisely five o'clock, but so far, Walter sat alone on a low bench, tapping his foot on the concrete. He checked his watch. 5:12 it read. It wasn't like Wendy to be late, and fear began to percolate in his gut. Attempting to ignore the 'what ifs' that were running through his mind, he lifted his head and observed the garden in the center of the square. This bit of green smack-dab in the middle of a grey, city street was truly a wonder.

"Hallo, Walt," Wendy said, dropping to the bench next to him.

Walter jumped. "Oh! I didn't see you coming."

"I wondered if you'd notice," she laughed. "I came from over the—," she said, stopping short as she pointed to the entrance on the Northwest corner.

Her eyes were wide. "Walter, what on earth—"

"D'you like it?" he asked, smiling broadly.

"I—it's just that—well you look like a completely different person," she stammered.

"I haven't quite gotten used to my reflection," he laughed.

"It looks good, though, Walt," she said, still inspecting his face.

"Thank you," he said, finding himself taking on an air of formality that seemed inappropriate and necessary all at once. "Shall we?" he asked, motioning toward the street.

"Sure," Wendy agreed hesitantly, lifting herself from the bench.

Walter couldn't quite put his finger on it, but she seemed...bouncier. More energetic? There had definitely been a change in her demeanor, and it was unsettling.

"So," Wendy sighed as they walked to the corner, "how've you been?"

"Only a few days have passed, but it feels like it's been...months," he admitted. "I've set up my flat and found a suitable local market. It's just down the street from my building."

"I know," Wendy gushed. "Isn't that one of the best things about this city? There's no need for a car! Everything is within walking distance."

"It is quite a lot of walking," Walter said.

"But easier than going to the gym," she said with a knowing glance.

"What's that supposed to mean?" Walter asked, his feathers ruffled. "I went twice a week that year—"

"I know," Wendy laughed. "I was only teasing. I'm the one who didn't take advantage of our membership, it wasn't *all* you. But it does seem more..." she gesticulated with her hands, searching for the words. "More organic, yeah? If we're getting our exercise during our day-to-day activities instead of having to take time out of our day—" she paused, and her hands fell to her sides. "I'm rambling, sorry," she said. "I'm really excited to be more active, that's all."

"It makes sense," Walter said. "It's a good point."

Wendy blushed. "I met a new friend at the pub last night," she said.

Walter immediately stiffened. "A friend?" he asked.

"She's a young thing, but she just arrived in Paris for her studies and doesn't know anyone either. Since we're both new, we decided to meet for supper a few times a week. You know, support each other a bit?"

"Sounds wonderful," Walter said, much more relaxed than he was a moment before. They approached Boulevard Saint Michel, and Walter turned to his wife. "You said you enjoy walking?"

She nodded.

"I thought we could walk around Saint Chappelle and—if you're up for it—all the way to Pont Neuf."

"Hmmm," Wendy said, tapping her lip with her index finger. "What's the distance?"

"Approximately 1.1 kilometers," Walter answered, glad that he'd mapped it out beforehand.

"So 2.2 back to this spot?" she asked.

"Technically, 2.2 kilometers back to the bench we were sitting on," Walter corrected.

"Sounds perfectly doable," she nodded, "and I actually haven't been that direction yet."

"Excellent," Walter said, leading her across the street. "I wondered if you'd had any time to sight-see already."

"A little," she said, "but not much."

"We'll be passing quite a few supper options on the way, so I thought we could stop when we're hungry."

"Sounds lovely," Wendy nodded.

Walter instinctively reached out to wrap his hand around hers but stopped short. It'd been a long time since they went on a walk holding hands, and he wasn't sure if that was something she'd welcome, given the situation. He determined to err on the side of caution and keep his hands to himself.

. . .

Walter leaned on the stone railing, looking out over the Seine. The light breeze felt lovely after their walk, especially since it had almost gotten up to thirty degrees Celsius in the afternoon and the evening was barely cooling down. Wendy stood next to him, her arms folded across her midsection while her dark hair blew lightly against her fair skin. Walter had always thought she was pretty. Her plump cheeks and narrow nose combined with the dimple in her left cheek always gave the impression that she was amused by something she wasn't willing or able to share. Tonight, he found himself wishing she would.

"Can you imagine this place before it was updated? When all the shops were still here?"

"I didn't know there used to be shops," Walter mused.

"It was a long time ago," she sighed. "But just imagine. The music, the art—"

"The pick-pockets," Walter said, immediately regretting it.

Wendy's jaw clenched and she turned away from him.

"Wendy, I was only—"

"No," she shook her head. "It's always something negative with you," she said, her tone more exhausted than angry.

"It was a joke," he said gently.

"Maybe it was, but the fact that your brain immediately goes there—" she paused, closing her eyes and taking a deep breath. "Sometimes that negativity is like a rope—attached to my ankles and whenever I start to rise, it yanks me right back down again," she said under her breath.

Her feelings were another blow to Walter's already fragile ego. He chose his words carefully.

"I'm not trying to pull you down, Wendy. To me, I guess it seems...pointless to spend all day with my head in the clouds when it isn't accomplishing anything."

"But who says it isn't, Walt? You?" she said, reeling on him. "What if that's where I gain happiness? Or where I might be inspired to do something—even if it is frivolous! Just once I would love for you to let me be there—"

"So you can be disappointed? Those dreams—" he stopped short.

"What?" she asked, her eyes flashing. "Those dreams—" she started him off, gesturing for him to finish.

Walter shook his head.

"I know you think that all of this is a waste of time, but I tried your way, Walter. It didn't work for me," she said, patting his arm and walking back in the direction of Place Dauphin. Walter turned his head and tried to lose himself in the sparkling blue expanse before him.

Chapter Seventeen

DECEMBER, 1987

Walter stood on the street, his feet numb from the cold as he stared at the display in the shop window. He'd heard Wendy talk multiple times with Mary about wanting a trenchcoat, and though it was out of season, Walter had found the exact style he thought she was looking for based on his eavesdropping. He'd walked past this window three times in the last week, but hadn't yet stepped over the threshold.

Just by the display, he knew the coat would be far out of his price range. Though he'd been working with a firm for the past eight months, he was still the low man on the totem pole. Until he wrote his exams in the spring, there wasn't any justification for a pay raise, even though their rent increased in September.

When Wendy brought up the idea of starting a family on the weekend, Walter nearly keeled over with heart palpitations. He could barely provide for the two of them, let alone a third human being thrown in the mix. Wendy had argued that she wouldn't lose any income; after her maternity leave, she'd plan to go back to work. She said it'd be good for her to not be stuck in the house all day, but Walter knew better.

He'd seen her with other people's babies and if that was any indication of the love and attachment she'd feel for their own child, he knew it would rip her apart to have to leave all day.

He wasn't ready for any of it. To know he'd be responsible for either fully providing for a family or breaking his wife's heart by requiring her to put food on the table. They wouldn't be able to afford their current flat regardless, which meant he'd either be commuting or looking for a different job. Which made all of the work he was currently putting in rather pointless. He'd only have to start over at the next firm. More hours, less pay.

Walter sighed, wiggling his toes to prevent them from getting stiff. The bell on the shop door jingled as a man stepped onto the sidewalk.

"Sir?" he said, addressing Walter.

"Yes?" Walter said, startled by the sudden attention.

"I'm sorry, sir, but I couldn't help but notice—you've been standing outside my window all week. Is there something I can help you with?"

"Just admiring this coat, that's all," Walter said. "It's almost Christmas."

"Glad to hear it. I'd started to wonder whether you were casing the place," the older man laughed nervously.

"I'd only be interested in stealing this if I were," Walter joked, quickly realizing the shop owner didn't find it funny. "No, I'd never—you see," he stammered, "my wife—we've been married just over a year—she's been mooning over a new coat for months, but we don't have a lot of money at the moment. I've been figuring a way to get it for her."

"Unsuccessfully, I assume?" the man asked.

"Right," Walter nodded. "So then I end up...staring. And

thinking. I'm sorry to have bothered you," he said, turning to trudge up the street in the dirty snow.

"Wait a second," the man called after him. "You may as well come in and take a look. I might have something inside that could work. Possibly at a lower price point."

Walter paused, turning again toward the shop. "I don't think you fully understand how low my price point would have to be," he said, shoving his hands in his coat pockets.

The man beckoned him inside. "At least you could warm up a bit," he said, and Walter didn't argue with that.

On Christmas morning, Wendy woke early and quietly tiptoed down the stairs. She pulled a skillet from the cupboard and set it on the stove, then reached into the fridge for the eggs and sausage she'd purchased the day before. She knew how much Walter loved a hot breakfast and today she planned to surprise him.

Once the pan was hot, she placed the sausages on the hot surface and they immediately began to sizzle. While they cooked, she prepared two place settings on their small table and filled the tea kettle with water.

Walter trundled down the stairs as she was cracking the eggs.

"What on earth are you doing up so early?" he asked, yawning.

"I'm making you breakfast," she grinned proudly, barely meeting his eyes before stretching her hands to the sink to rinse the raw egg from her fingers.

"Smells wonderful," he said, walking up behind her and wrapping his arms around her waist.

"It's almost ready," she laughed, pulling away from him before he could kiss her neck. "Let's eat and then we can open presents."

Walter sighed.

"What?" Wendy asked, bringing the plate of sausages to the table.

"Nothing," Walter said.

"I heard that sigh. I know something's wrong, so out with it," she insisted.

"Nothing's wrong, per se, I just wonder if this Christmas feels...underwhelming to you?" Walter asked hesitantly.

"Why, because we're on our own?"

He nodded. "Last year we were with your parents and..." he paused, turning to look under their waist-high tree covered in tinsel and small, sparkly lights. "It's fairly sparse."

Wendy smiled. "I'm not worried about the number of presents, if that's what you're getting at. I'm glad to be spending this holiday with you in our very own home."

"You're sure?" Walter asked, pulling out his chair and taking a seat.

"Absolutely positive," she said resolutely.

They ate heartily and then moved the few meters to the living room with giddy anticipation. Walter insisted that Wendy open her present first. As she peeled back the layer of decorative wrapping paper, her eyes lit up. Then, pulling the trench coat from its box, her expression seemed to dampen.

"It's lovely," she said, lifting it out to have a look. "Thank you, Walt."

"You don't like it," he said, deflating.

"No, I love it," she said, "it's just—well, initially I was thinking a three-quarter length would be more flattering, but looking at this—I think it's perfect."

She smiled as she folded it back up and set it next to the chair.

"Well?" she said. "Aren't you going to open yours?"

Walter nodded, forcing a happy expression to his face. As he picked up his box, all he could think about was how long it was going to take him to pay off the coat. When he'd bought it, the anticipated look on her face was more than enough to compensate for the risk he felt at buying something on credit.

He shook his head lightly as he began to open Wendy's gift to him. His expectations were the problem, he thought, chastising himself internally. He should've waited until Wendy specifically told him what she wanted. Next year, he'd do better.

Chapter Eighteen

LATE MAY, 2014

"Is this a good time?" Wendy asked, settling into the sofa, tucking her right leg under her.

"Perfect," Mary said on the other end of the line.

"I'm sorry we haven't connected until now," Wendy apologized. "Every time I thought to call it was either too late or too early," she laughed. "You'd think that being in a closer timezone we'd be able to connect more easily."

"I've been swamped the last few days, so I likely wouldn't have had time to chat anyway," Mary said. "I'm dying to hear about Paris, though. Fill me in."

"It's incredible, Mar. There's so much energy here. I feel like I could do anything. Be anyone, you know?"

"You seem different even over the phone," Mary laughed. "You sound...alive."

"That's precisely how I feel! Every street corner I find something new and exciting. New foods, new artists, new styles. I've started a list," she said hesitantly.

"What kind of a list?"

"It sounds silly, but I call it my 'Paris Dreams' list," Wendy said.

"Go on..."

"It's a list of all my dreams for the next three months, along with steps I can take to reach them."

"Give me an example," Mary said.

"Alright, just a moment," Wendy said, hopping off the couch to retrieve her list from the counter. "Ah," she said, scanning the first column. "Here's one I've been checking off easily: 'Try something new each day,' oh!" she exclaimed, "This is a harder one, but I've checked it off partially: 'Meet new friends.'" She returned to the sofa, this time resting her head on the pillow and letting her legs hang loosely over the side.

"You've made friends already?" Mary said in surprise.

"I said partially," Wendy laughed. "I invited a young woman to join my table the other night and we hit it off. She's a student here and needed a friend, as well."

"I was hoping it would be a tall, handsome man of the French variety..." Mary teased.

"Okay, right, because a tall, handsome man would most definitely be interested in a soon-to-be-divorced, middle-aged, menopausal woman with emotional baggage."

"It makes you mysterious," Mary laughed. "And you're underselling yourself. You're quite pretty."

Wendy scoffed. "Well, not a tall, handsome Gerard. Sorry to disappoint."

"You had a date with Walter, yes?"

"It was earlier this evening," she sighed. "We took a nice walk."

"That was it?"

"We were supposed to get dinner, but we stopped on a beautiful bridge and started talking—I thought it was a fairly benign topic—but Walter managed to poo-poo it within minutes. I ended up leaving and picking up a crépe on the way back to my flat."

"You have to do two dates a week?"

"That's the deal."

"Are you going to be able to handle that?" Mary asked skeptically.

"I get to plan the next one. I fancy the idea of choosing places Walter would absolutely hate," Wendy said, and Mary laughed out loud.

"D'you think I'm a terrible person?" Wendy asked, giggling mischievously.

"Absolutely not," Mary said, taking a breath. "I wish I could be there."

"I won't make it too miserable for him. But maybe just a little bit of fun is warranted."

"Are you just toying with him, then?" Mary asked.

"What do you mean?"

"With these three months. Do you have any intention of changing your mind?"

"This wasn't my idea, if you recall. Walter was the one who suggested—"

"I know, I wasn't trying to accuse you," Mary cut in. "But if you're not planning to change your mind...don't you think you ought to tell the poor fellow?"

"I think I've made it abundantly clear in our past conversations."

"But clearly he hasn't gotten the message. He's still holding out hope."

Wendy sighed, rubbing her eyes. "I know," she said softly. "So you think I should be honest with him?"

"It's up to you. I do feel a bit bad for the bloke."

"I'll think about it," Wendy said. "But enough about me, how are things going for you?"

"Same old," she said, then paused for dramatic effect, "though I do have a date next weekend."

"That is absolutely not 'same old,'" Wendy said excitedly. "How'd you meet?"

She listened as Mary filled her in on all the details for nearly half an hour. This man had helped her on the tube when she lost her balance—a classic, completely cheesy meet-cute. It did make her slightly nervous that Mary knew very little about him and was unconcerned about meeting one-on-one...though they were meeting at a public coffee shop. She opted not to share her reservations with her obviously elated friend.

"Wonderful," she said, yawning. "Can't wait to hear how it goes."

"You need sleep," Mary laughed. "Let's connect later in the week?"

"I'll ring you Friday," Wendy said, and they quickly said their heartfelt goodbyes.

Chapter Nineteen

Walter woke the morning after their Wednesday date much too early. He hadn't slept well, for obvious reasons, and his body felt tense and unsettled. So far, this experiment was *not* going the way he'd anticipated. He had assumed that being in Paris and making an effort—when he apparently hadn't been for the last who knows how many years—would change Wendy's mind. And most importantly, her heart. Could it really be too late? Could he have damaged things so irreparably that there was no going back?

These thoughts left an emptiness in his chest that was so sickening, he couldn't lie still any longer. He had to do something to rid himself of the stew of emotions bubbling up in his being, but what? Feeling desperate, he glanced down at his trainers protruding from beneath the bed. Without thinking, he quickly changed into a pair of joggers and a t-shirt, pulled the rarely used shoes onto his feet, and double knotted the laces.

At exactly 6:05 in the morning, Walter Winslow embarked on his first outdoor run in nearly twenty years. In Paris, no less. Within the first block, his lungs screamed for air and he quite nearly gave up, but the anger, frustration, and deep sadness within him demanded that he continue. He pressed on, gasping and sweating profusely, until by the fourth block, he found that his heart no longer felt like it was going to explode. It still didn't feel comfortable by any means, but gratefully, he was sure he wasn't going to die. Not right at this moment, at least.

A few more blocks and Walter's right knee began to ache. Checking his watch, he saw that he'd been running for over fifteen minutes. While he didn't know his relative speed, and therefore couldn't determine his distance, he did know that he likely had gone over a mile. That, in and of itself, felt like a monumental accomplishment and, since he didn't want to injure himself, he slowed his pace to a fast walk. His knee stopped complaining—less impact on the pavement, he supposed.

His body hummed, vibrating with energy he hadn't known existed anymore. And, most importantly, he no longer felt like crawling in a hole and hiding from the world. Remembering advice from his college years, he allowed his body to cool down by walking another few blocks, then stopped between two shops to stretch. Even last week, he never would have felt comfortable drawing so much attention to himself by assuming strange positions on the side of the street, but today? He'd run a mile, maybe more, for goodness' sake. He couldn't have cared less what passersby thought of him. And that felt incredible.

As he stretched his calves by pressing his toes up against the wall, one leg at a time, he looked left and noticed the shop next to him was a café. Obviously he'd never seen it before since it was quite a ways from his flat, but as it was now breakfast time and he had just exerted an abnormal amount of energy, he couldn't resist. Though he was still flushed and damp with sweat, he walked through the door.

A few bistro tables with chairs sat in the corner, but Walter ignored them and approached the counter to place his order. His French was so-so, but he successfully ordered a pain au chocolat pastry and two boiled eggs, along with a small glass of orange juice. He waited for the woman behind the counter to assemble his breakfast on a plate, then retrieved them from the counter, thanked her, and turned to the tables he had passed.

A sophisticated woman with tortoiseshell glasses and grey hair curling under her jaw line sat alone at the table by the window. Not wanting to interrupt, Walter chose the table closest to the entrance, sitting with his back to the door. All morning he'd felt the urge to smooth his moustache, and this moment was no exception. As his hand raised to his now bare lip, he caught himself and instead reached for his napkin, placing it on his lap. He had just begun to salt and pepper his eggs when a voice caught his attention.

"I'd be 'appy to share the window," the woman said behind him, and Walter turned. "Vous sont American, no?"

Walter pointed at his chest. "Me?" he asked, somewhat startled. "Yes, I'm American. Well, actually, I'm British," he explained puffing out his chest, "but I've lived in America for the past fifteen years or so."

She raised her eyebrow, her eyes drifting down to his t-shirt and joggers.

"Yes, well," Walter muttered. "I guess this is quite American of me. I was running and then decided to grab a bite—"

She waved him off, laughing, then motioned for him to take the seat closer to her near the window.

"Eating alone is only satisfying when you 'ave people to watch," she said with a smirk.

"It does make things more interesting," Walter agreed, shifting to the table next to hers. "I'm Walter Winslow," he said.

"Genevieve," she answered, nodding.

They sat in silence, watching men and women bustling along the streets. They both chuckled audibly when a young man ripped his trousers as he attempted to squeeze between another pedestrian and a bicycle. When he was finished eating, Walter returned his plate to the counter and walked to the door.

"Thanks for the view, Genevieve," he said.

"Ciao," she said nonchalantly with a small nod in his direction.

Stepping out on the street, Walter began walking back the way he came with newfound confidence and extremely sore legs.

Chapter Twenty

This time, Wendy asked for a table for two when she approached the hostess. It seemed slightly wrong to be eating at a Canadian restaurant in Paris, but Cami seemed overly excited at the prospect of having wings, so The Moose, it was. The restaurant was surprisingly jam-packed at seven o'clock on a Friday night. Though there was a slight wait, Wendy didn't mind. Cami hadn't arrived yet and, like Mary had commented, she felt alive simply absorbing the energy around her.

She waited in the corner of the entrance, surreptitiously glancing at the patrons seated at the wooden tables, attempting to predict who would leave first. Her best guess was the group of friends along the south wall. They were engaged in jovial conversation, but their plates had long been clean and their glasses empty.

The door swung open and Cami entered the restaurant wearing a red cotton shirt, but otherwise looking exactly as she had the first time they met. Wendy smiled broadly.

"Bonsoir," Cami said with a churlish grin.

"Ah, are we practicing our French this evening?" Wendy asked, amused.

"Nope," Cami said resolutely. "My brain is completely fried. That's the only thing I could manage," she laughed.

"Fine by me," Wendy said. "We've got a tad bit of a wait."

"No problem," Cami said, moving next to her. "I was looking at the reviews online for this place. The food looks amazing."

"I'm predicting acid reflux as I lie down for bed in a few hours," Wendy said.

Cami waved her off. "Sometimes it's worth it, Wendy. You need to live a little."

"I think I'm doing plenty of living!" Wendy exclaimed. "But I live a lot better when my esophagus isn't burning."

"Always so practical," Cami teased good-humoredly.

Her comment stopped Wendy in her proverbial tracks. Practical? Practical was Walter's specialty, *not* hers. She was a dreamer. She was anything *but* practical. Taking care of one's body and avoiding negative physical consequences wasn't a refusal to let loose, but merely a strategy to create more 'living' opportunities in the future.

"Hey," Cami said, reaching out and resting her hand on Wendy's arm. "Are you okay?"

"Mmhmm," Wendy answered, shaking her head.

"I was kidding, I didn't mean—"

"No," Wendy said, "I know. It was...I was thinking of something else for a moment."

Cami nodded, but concern still creased her face.

"I'm fine!" Wendy laughed. "It was just a reminder of my age, that's all. I used to be able to eat fried foods to my heart's content. Things become a little less worth it when you know you're going to feel terrible afterwards."

"That should be my new life mantra," Cami sighed, and Wendy laughed out loud.

"You're young! How could you possibly be living with regrets already?"

"I'm not that young," Cami said with a hand on her hip.

"Madame?" a voice sounded, and both women turned their attention to the host. "Your table is ready," he said, his accent thick.

Wendy nodded gratefully, and they followed him to a table near the back of the room. It was not the spot Wendy had predicted. That group was still going strong. They sat and slung their purses over the backs of their chairs.

"It's not that I'm living my life with regrets," Cami said, continuing with her earlier train of thought, "it's more that...life isn't how I thought it was going to be."

"What do you mean?" Wendy asked, perusing the menu.

"I don't know? I guess I thought that by the time I was here—not here in Paris, but here at twenty-five—that I'd know exactly who I was and where I was headed. I still have no clue!" she exclaimed, then paused, inspecting the table. "And it's terrifying."

"Or exciting," Wendy said. "By the time I was your age, I *did* have a plan splayed out in front of me, and I followed it exactly. I can tell you from experience, it didn't help me understand who I was, nor did it prevent me from feeling like I hadn't a clue what I was doing."

"Your path was a family?"

"It was," Wendy nodded, "And I'm not saying—"

Their waiter approached their table, asking if they'd prefer still or sparkling water. Cami suggested they order, considering how busy they were, so Wendy inspected the menu with increased fervor.

"I'll take...the Moose Bowl," Wendy said.

"Want to share a poutine?" Cami asked excitedly.

"Sure, you choose," she said.

"Ummmm, we'll take the Classic," Cami said, smiling appreciatively and handing the menu to him.

As he retreated, Cami turned her attention back to Wendy. "Sorry, you got cut off," she said.

"No, it's alright. What were we talking about?"

"Your path. Family," Cami reminded gently.

"Right," Wendy nodded, taking a deep breath. "I'm only saying that having a sure course has its own tradeoffs. I remember feeling exactly the way you describe. Worrying about where life would take me and if I'd see 'success,' whatever that means. But I guess that's my point," she said pointedly. "We have all these expectations and judgements about what 'success' is and then we're disappointed when things aren't linear. But linear has its own cost."

Cami sighed, crossing her arms and leaning back in her chair. "I guess. It would be so much easier if I just *knew*, you know? How it was going to end up?"

Wendy laughed, clapping her hands together. "No! That's exactly my point!" she exclaimed. "There's no 'ending up.' I 'ended up' married with two lovely children—the perfect life, right? And yet here I am. Alone in Paris, approaching a divorce and a new beginning."

Cami's head cocked to one side. "Is that why you're here?"

Wendy cleared her throat, sobering immediately. "I guess we didn't get into that last time," she said. "Right. Well, yes. I'm here because my soon-to-be-ex-husband wanted to give our marriage one last shot," she said dramatically. "I asked for a divorce a few months back. He somehow thinks that being here and...dating again," she said rolling her eyes.

"He wants to date you in Paris?"

"Ugh, don't give me that look," Wendy groaned.

"You have to admit. It is kind of romantic," Cami said, raising an eyebrow.

"It would be if I hadn't spent a quarter of a century saying 'yes, Walter' and 'anything you like, Walter' and setting aside everything that I've wanted in my life to keep him comfortable," Wendy said, raising her voice and drawing the attention of both tables next to them.

"I'm sorry," Cami said gently, reaching across the table and patting Wendy's hand. "So what do you recommend?" she asked, her eyebrows drawn together. "It's kind of a cruel irony, right? I can't enjoy where I'm at, because I don't know anything different. But you *do* know different...and you're not really enjoying it either," she said with a sardonic laugh. "I don't know. This whole 'life' thing is complicated."

Wendy laughed out loud, but kept her volume low this time. "That it is. And you're right. I don't have any good answers, Cami. All I know is that standing on the other side of 'known' and 'predictable,' I think I'd like to have taken more risks."

"It's good advice," Cami nodded. "And it's not like I have any control over it anyway," she laughed mirthlessly. "I may as well *choose* volatility instead of lamenting it."

"That's the spirit," Wendy laughed, picking up the fresh glass of still water that had just appeared at the table and pressing it to her lips.

The food was, indeed, quite good as Cami had promised, but the view that evening turned out to be even better. Wendy had gotten used to being in such close proximity with other diners in Paris over the past few weeks and was quite adept at ignoring the people next to her. Tonight, however, she and Cami were both finding it difficult to stay focused.

After their food had arrived, two men had been seated next to them. Two very attractive French men. Their dark features, fashionable haircuts, and five 0'clock shadows combined with crisp business casual attire was almost too much for Cami to handle. She stared at Wendy, nodding her head ever so slightly in their direction until Wendy had taken a glance.

The men were so close—and there was no guarantee that they couldn't understand English—that the women weren't able to talk about it until they walked out the door of the establishment.

"He was looking at you!" Wendy burst out as soon as they were on the street.

Cami laughed, doubling over to catch her breath. "That. Was. The most uncomfortable half-hour I've experienced in a long time," she said, standing upright. "I couldn't even think! All I could see was this gorgeous face in my peripheral vision."

"I loved watching you try to stay focused," Wendy grinned.

"Oh don't start," Cami teased. "I saw you sneaking glances every two seconds."

"I don't know what you're talking about," Wendy laughed. "It's easier for me because I know there's no chance someone like that would be interested in someone like...this," she said, motioning to herself.

"Not true," Cami insisted. "You're not giving yourself enough credit."

"Men like that are interested in young things like yourself," Wendy said as they walked along the street.

"Not all of them. You're really pretty, Wendy, and you're confident. You've got great style—"

"Ha!" Wendy exclaimed. "I don't even know what my style is! I bought this because I saw someone else wearing something similar and it seemed like it would help me look...less American. But I've been putting off new clothes because I don't want to be this size much longer," she said, motioning to her midsection. "Does that sound like confidence to you?"

Cami sighed. "We all have insecurities," she said. "But

you're out living your life. Taking risks, like you said. That's attractive to men."

Wendy shrugged her shoulders. "Where are we even going?" she asked, turning to Cami. "Don't you live in the opposite direction?"

They both burst out laughing as Cami nodded.

"Thanks for tonight," she said when she was able to talk normally. "Next week?"

Wendy smiled, giving a wave as Cami turned back the way they came.

Chapter Twenty-One

MAY, 1992

"What would you think about a holiday next month?" Wendy asked excitedly. She'd given Walter plenty of time to rest after returning home from work, and both boys were fast asleep, though Darrel would likely be waking up to nurse in another hour or so.

"Next month?" Walter asked, lifting his eyes from the pages of his book. "I'm not sure that'll work."

"It's still a month off from your busy time," Wendy countered. "And we've saved a nice little nest egg—"

"Little is right," Walter said, looking back to his book. "I'd love a holiday as much as the next bloke, but have you crunched the numbers on how much we need to save to retire, let alone cover the expenses of our children as they grow up?"

"I haven't—no," Wendy stammered, her brow furrowing. "But surely we could—"

"It's astronomical," Walter continued. "I think we'd better wait until we have at least..."

Walter continued on, but Wendy stopped listening after

his emphatic 'no.' He didn't have to say the word for her to understand there wasn't going to be any more discussion on the topic. She loved how dedicated he was to providing for their family and how hard he worked so she could be at home with the boys. Going back to work when Calvin was a year old had crushed her, and when Darrel came along, she couldn't imagine leaving them both. Especially not for a job she didn't particularly care for.

"Walt," she said, realizing he had stopped talking. "I'm worried you're working too hard. I know we need to save, but taking a break once in a while is good for the soul. And good for our family."

Walter again lifted his eyes from his book. "I do take breaks," he said gently. "I'm sitting in a recliner reading a book right this very moment."

"You know what I mean," Wendy said, placing a hand on her hip to accentuate her point.

"I do," he said, rising from his chair and setting his book on the coffee table. "I would like to take a holiday at some point, but right now? Why would we waste money on transportation and—and fancy food, accommodations? It's all a little frivolous when we have a perfectly good home and plenty of time to relax here without spending a cent, don't you think? When we've got a little more saved and I've worked my way up, we could consider something at that point," he offered.

Wendy nodded, attempting to hide her disappointment, but failing. Walter took her hand in his and slid his arm around her waist as he began rocking back and forth. Wendy loved dancing, and Walter knew it. He twirled her around the living room slowly at first, and then with more gusto.

Pulling her close, he whispered in her ear, "I only want to make sure we're taken care of."

"I know," Wendy whispered back. "I know."

Chapter Twenty-Two

Wendy lay in her bed staring at the ceiling. The moon shone brightly outside the window, bathing her small bedroom in pale light. She clutched the covers to her, breathing deeply as her mind raced. Cami had called her practical tonight, and the word clung to her like a dirty secret. No matter how hard she tried to erase the comment and the thoughts it created, it refused to release its claws.

And then there was the face of the man next to them. His full lips and broad shoulders. She found herself fantasizing about what it would be like to have a man like *that* interested in her. What if she wasn't ever able to find someone after all this? How did one meet someone when they weren't living the life of a young, college socialite?

Wendy couldn't sleep. Was she treating Cami the way Walter had treated her all these years? Crushing her dreams and grounding her instead of freely giving her belief? It wasn't like Wendy had much experience with Cami, and therefore, likely didn't have that kind of power. But clearly, Wendy's opinion *did* matter to the girl. Why did it feel so uncomfortable to say 'good for you' or 'you should go for it'? It's not like

Cami's dreams were bad—after all, they'd been Wendy's dreams, as well, when she was younger. Before she knew all that came with them.

Of course, Wendy knew it was possible to live out a marriage, raising a family, and keeping house without it feeling like a veritable prison. You only had to find the right partner. Someone who wouldn't allow you to lose yourself in it—someone who was looking out for you as much as you'd been looking out for them. So yes. She could support Cami in her dream, but possibly give a teensy bit of advice when it came to dating...and knowing a lot about life before ever settling down...

"Ugh!" Wendy groaned out loud throwing her legs out from under the covers. Why did this have to be so difficult!? She'd done everything right, hadn't she? Been the model daughter and member of enlightened society. Unless she'd waited until she was at least thirty, she'd never have had enough experience to make a decision fully knowing what was at stake. And even then...she'd probably have resented the fact that she hadn't found a partner or had a family yet. Even with perfect hindsight, she couldn't figure out where it had gone wrong or how things could've turned out differently.

As far as Cami was concerned, Wendy needed to shut her big, fat mouth. Her advice wasn't worth much considering her current situation, and it wasn't fair to lead the poor girl astray. She'd apologize in the morning. As for now, Wendy hopped from the bed and laid herself flat on the floor, stretched her arms over her head, and focused on her breath, mentally checking 'meditation' off her dreams list.

Chapter Twenty-Three

JUNE, 2014

Walter had visited his newly found cafe regularly over the last two weeks. He didn't run there, though he was still jogging most mornings. His unexpected initial foray into the world of running ignited something within him. Perhaps it was the complete lack of control in other areas of his life that made pushing himself each morning so appealing, but whatever the case, he was consistently running nearly twelve miles a week.

Though he hadn't stepped on a scale, he could already see and feel the difference in his body. His knee wasn't aching anymore, for one, and his pants were much looser than they had been a month ago. He felt accomplished—powerful—every time he walked through the door short of breath and drenched in sweat. It made the endless, empty days seem manageable.

He'd done all the sight-seeing one could possibly tolerate within a three-week period. After a while, each museum began to look the same; every architectural wonder blending into the next, and every priceless historical artifact seeming mundane and meaningless. The empty days were exactly why he'd been making the trek to that particular cafe, despite the fact that it was a long walk from his flat and he passed at least ten other suitable breakfast options before arriving. At *that* cafe, he found a small piece of everything he'd been seeking since arriving in Paris, albeit with someone quite unexpected.

Genevieve was nearly always seated in the window when he arrived before 6:30 in the morning. She didn't always stay for long, but for a French woman, she was surprisingly warm and welcoming. He had learned over the last few weeks she had been living in Paris for ten years. She moved to the city after selling her home in the French countryside following the unexpected death of her husband.

"Too lonely," she had explained with a dismissive wave of her hand. Now she worked as a copywriter—mostly from home, but sometimes at the cafe when she needed a change of scenery. Regardless, she never missed her morning cafe au lait and croissant with butter and marmalade.

This morning, Genevieve nodded as Walter walked through the door and pulled out the chair next to her. He'd frequented this establishment often enough that he no longer needed to put in an order at the counter. It would magically appear with a tab approximately ten minutes after his arrival. This was likely the part of the experience Walter treasured most. Each time his breakfast arrived, he felt important—like he belonged to a secret club.

"Bonjour," Genevieve said, taking a sip of her coffee.

"Bonjour," Walter greeted, a smile on his lips. "What's the news, then?"

At this, Genevieve rolled her eyes and began a lengthy diatribe in partial English—mostly French—about politics, land use permits, and historical preservation. If the automatic breakfast arrival was Walter's favorite, this part of the morning was second on his list. He understood approximately thirty percent of what she said, but her energy was intoxicating. She cared so much, and all Walter clung to was the hope that some of her caring would rub off on him. Because right now, this human connection was the only thing that kept him from sinking into the void of his own anxieties. Especially after last night with Wendy.

Walter nodded, bringing a piece of croissant to his lips. Genevieve sighed, her passion waning as she explained her final point. She leaned back in her chair, sweeping a section of silver hair behind her ear before taking a sip of coffee.

"Et tu?" she asked, offering him the chance to share. Normally, he didn't say much. Sometimes he'd update her on his children or talk about something he noticed on his morning run, but today was different. There was a conglomeration of discomfort wedged in his very soul that wouldn't let loose. Like a cancer of worry eating away at him from the inside. If he didn't lance it and release the pressure, he felt like he might explode.

"Have I told you...about my wife, Wendy?"

Genevieve leaned forward, her eyes intently focused. She shook her head.

"We've been married for twenty-eight years, but a couple of months ago—" Walter paused, clearing his throat. "She told me in no uncertain terms she wanted a divorce."

"Pourquoi?" Genevieve asked, her eyebrows furrowed.

"That's just it," Walter said, throwing up his hands. "It seemed to come out of nowhere. After discussing it at length, I became acutely aware of the fact that I've been making her feel stifled for years. She talks about wanting more excitement—living her dreams, but...I guess I've never really had any. Or at least not like the ones she talks about," he chuckled nervously. "I was happy. Our life was comfortable. Predictable."

Genevieve nodded. "She's itchy."

Walter stared at her, confused. "Come again?"

"Itchy," Genevieve repeated, stretching out her arms and moving her body as if shaking off discomfort.

"Oh!" Walter exclaimed, "you mean 'she's itching' for something. She's uncomfortable."

"Oui," Genevieve said, pleased with herself.

"I think you're right," Walter sighed, bringing his glass to his lips. "And I was too big a dolt to recognize it. Or even to think about her feelings once in a while. Truly, it never occurred to me that we could be having such different experiences," he explained.

Genevieve pulled the salt and pepper toward her, then placed her hand vertically between the two jars, creating a wall.

Walter nodded again, tears stinging the corners of his eyes. "We haven't talked about anything that really matters in years," he said softly. "I was complacent, and now...I might lose her forever," he said, wiping a tear from his cheek. "We're trying again—three months, two dates a week—but I can tell her heart's not in it. She took me to the gardens last night and she talked about the plants, growing seasons, and everything else she's learned about French horticulture," he laughed, shaking his head, "but not *once* did she show interest in me. Or her life with me. I think she's *actually* moving on. And leaving me behind—"

At this, Walter lost any semblance of control over his emotions and began to openly weep. He buried his face in his hands, knowing full-well that an outburst like this was very un-French.

Chapter Twenty-Four

The next day, Walter showered and dressed, readying himself to meet Wendy at the Tuileries Gardens for their first visit to the Musée d'Orsay and possibly a pop-in to see the water lilies at the Musée de l'Orangerie. Walter planned this one knowing how much Wendy loved impressionist and post-impressionist art. Though he wasn't as moved by art museums as she, today needed to be special. The setting needed to be as perfect and joyful as possible for him to have the courage to go through with his plan. He'd been concocting all sorts of scenarios for days and this seemed to be the most fitting.

Walter pulled the tags off a new pair of leather shoes he'd found shopping yesterday. With all of the running he'd been doing—and despite the croissants—he'd gone down two trouser sizes and was forced to buy new clothing. His old wardrobe sat forlorn in his suitcase. Though it was no longer needed at this point, Walter was hesitant to part with it since he wasn't convinced this new size would last. Purchasing new clothes and then having to buy *more* if he gained the weight back sounded quite frivolous.

Since he'd been the same weight for over ten years, he was almost positive that as soon as he got back to America, his body would settle into homeostasis. Though...he didn't want it to. He quite enjoyed this new look and, more importantly, how he felt. He hadn't suffered from a headache in nearly two weeks, and every night he slept like a baby—no more tossing and turning at midnight. He regularly pondered on how he could keep his new habits upon returning home but found himself at a loss.

His phone buzzed and he walked to the counter to pick it up.

"Calvin," he said joyfully, holding the phone to his ear. "To what do I owe this pleasure?"

"What, I'm not allowed to call and check in on you for no reason?"

"You're allowed, but I'm not sure that's ever happened. Usually, you call your mum," he chuckled.

Calvin laughed. "I tried her, actually, but she didn't pick up."

"Aha," Walter teased.

"Is she there with you?" Calvin asked.

Walter cleared his throat. "No, but I'm about to meet her for lunch. Do you need me to pass a message along?"

"Becky and I—we've been trying to get a hold of you because we wanted to share the gender of the baby," Calvin said.

"Oh, that's wonderful," Walter said, a smile lighting up his face. "Why don't I call you right back when we're together. Wait...isn't it five-thirty in the morning over there?"

"It is," Calvin sighed.

"And it's Saturday."

"Mmhmm. Becky hasn't been sleeping well. She wakes up and then can't get back to sleep. I heard her rummaging around in the kitchen," he said, yawning. "We'll probably eat something and then go back to bed for a few hours."

"I remember those days," Walter muttered, feeling for his son. "I'll call as soon as I can."

"Thanks, Dad. And I really would love to hear how you're doing."

"Same old, same old," Walter said. "You know me."

"Love you," Calvin said. "Talk soon."

As soon as Walter caught Wendy's figure moving toward him, he rushed to her and explained the situation. They found a somewhat quiet spot—not an easy feat on a Saturday afternoon—and quickly dialed Calvin's number.

"Mum? Dad?"

"We're here, Cal," Wendy said excitedly.

She looked radiant in a floral skirt and pale pink blouse, as if she planned to match the artist's work they were about to admire. Walter's eyes wandered from her bright eyes to the creases around her mouth, moving and changing with each smile.

"Walter, come closer so you can hear," she said, motioning with her hands.

"We went to our ultrasound last week and we wanted to come up with some way to share the news that wasn't…as boring as this," Calvin laughed.

"I wanted to send a letter with glitter," Becky jumped in, "but Cal said Walter would murder me."

Wendy and Walter laughed out loud.

"Thanks, Cal," Walter said.

"Anyway, we figured we just needed to tell you, so here it is," Calvin said, then both of them shouted, "We're having a boy!"

Wendy squealed with delight and Walter's cheeks flushed with pride. A grandson. Their first grandson.

"Wonderful news," Wendy said. "We would've been thrilled either way, of course, but a son. That's fantastic, you two."

"Congratulations," Walter cut in. "You must be chuffed."

"We are, Dad. Thanks," Calvin said. "Anyway, we don't want to interrupt your lunch. Thanks for calling back."

"Thanks for trying to get a hold of us," Wendy gushed.

"Back to bed then, eh?" Walter said.

"We're already there," Becky laughed. "No plans today, so we can sleep as long as we want."

After a few goodbyes from each of them, Wendy ended the call and slipped her phone into her handbag.

"A grandson," she said under her breath. "Shall we?" she said, looking back toward the street. "I've heard good things about that place," she said, motioning to a restaurant on the end of the block. "You look good, Walt. Have you lost weight?" she asked flippantly as she passed.

"Lead the way," Walter said, a deep sadness permeating his being as he followed her down the walk.

After enjoying a lunch of roast chicken and pomme frites, Walter and Wendy entered the museum. Though they waited briefly for security, they were able to skip most of the line with their Paris pass. Darrel had researched that for them, and it was the gift that kept on giving.

Once inside, they marveled at the domed, glass ceiling of the old railway station and were quickly taken in by the statues adorning the main corridor. Wendy stopped at each one, and Walter tried to find meaning in them the way he knew she was. He had decided during lunch that he would wait until the very end of their time together to talk with Wendy. Until then, he'd attempt to enjoy her companionship and the beautiful works that adorned the walls around them.

Each room they ducked into offered something new, and Walter found himself using his phone to search the history and backstory of specific pieces that struck him. Though, to be fair, he wasn't exactly in a position to focus wholly on the masterpieces in front of him. He kept watching Wendy's purse, cursing the fact that she'd brought the leather one with a zipper on top. He touched the envelope in his jacket pocket every so often, hoping he'd be able to succeed in slipping it into her bag without her notice. He didn't think he had the strength to hand it to her openly, given what he planned to do.

Eventually, they made it to the back and ascended the stairs to the impressionist section. Wendy had been patient, but now was almost shaking with anticipation. Using great restraint—or being desperately thirsty—she turned to take a drink from the fountain near the bathroom before walking toward the entrance. Wiping a drip of water that traveled down her chin, she returned to where Walter waited for her and unzipped her purse. She took out a tube of balm and quickly applied it to her lips. As she replaced it, she carelessly threw her bag over her shoulder, leaving it partially open. Walter seized his opportunity—taking advantage of her distraction as they approached the door—and quickly tucked the envelope into the now open space, watching as it fell deeper into her purse with each step.

Feeling quite accomplished and relieved, Walter trailed his wife as they entered the space. They obediently followed the line clockwise as the works of Renoir, Degas, and Cezanne immediately overtook their senses. Though he was somewhat familiar with these artists, seeing their brushstrokes in the flesh left Walter awestruck. Wendy couldn't stop whispering to him little-known facts and interpretations of each painting they passed, but by the time they reached their first Manet, Walter turned to her.

"I think I'm going to take a moment on that bench," he said quietly. Wendy nodded her approval, though her face showed concern.

"I'm alright, just need a break," he said, ducking out of the flow of traffic. He sat on the bench and realized he had a surprisingly good view of a gorgeous Monet to his left. Swiveling, he reveled in the relative silence around him and the swirling colors on the canvas in front of him.

He wasn't sure how long he'd been sitting there before Wendy joined him.

Following his gaze, she said, "It's beautiful, isn't it?"

Walter nodded.

"Great idea coming here," she said. "Do you think we should save d'Orangerie for another time?"

"Wendy..." Walter said, his voice faltering. "I'm fairly spent for today. But, I don't think I'll be going with you another time, though I do hope you make it. I've heard the oval rooms alone are worth the visit."

Wendy's eyebrows furrowed. "What do you mean you don't think you'll be going?" she asked in genuine confusion.

Walter sucked in a breath, held it for a second, and let it out slowly. "I'm becoming ardently aware that you were serious," he said, turning and meeting her eyes. "Though I don't want to admit it to myself or anyone else, I can see that you truly want a life that's different from the one we've built."

Walter's heart started to race, and he wiped his hands on his trousers. "I'm going to head home. On Monday," he said. "That way you can enjoy your last months—or however long you end up staying—and you won't need to worry about me or our dates. You'll be free to do what you please. Then, when you're ready we can talk about what comes next."

Wendy stared at him. "Where is this coming from?" she

asked softly. "You were adamant that we needed to give this three months—"

"But that was me not listening again, wasn't it?" he said with a soft smile. He patted her knee and stood up. "I think it's time for me to go home. Thanks for a lovely afternoon," he said, then turned and walked out the way they entered.

Chapter Twenty-Five

Though confused by Walter's sudden turnabout the evening before, Wendy couldn't say she was disappointed. Their dates were enjoyable, but they weren't accomplishing what she knew Walter had hoped they would, and that only made her feel guilty. It was more like spending time with an old friend.

Still, when the image of Walter walking glumly out of the room flashed through her mind during the day, she couldn't deny the sense of regret that accompanied it. She waffled back and forth about calling him and assuring him that she'd be happy to finish out the contract, but couldn't quite bring herself to do it.

That phone call would be partially motivated by assuaging that guilt, mixed with her incessant fear of being alone and pathetic self-doubt and desperation. It would not be motivated by a sincere desire to solve things between them, and definitely not by love. She had lived her life with fear of the unknown as a motivator for far too long. With Walter heading home, she'd feel far less shame about her plans for the day. He had given her his blessing to officially move on, and she was going to take it.

Last week, Wendy had encountered a man on one of her regular trips to the market. She'd seen him there before but hadn't the gumption previously to strike up a conversation. For whatever reason, that morning—as she'd been reaching for a fresh bunch of broccolini—she'd said hello. The word had tumbled out of her mouth and she'd blushed when he turned and smiled. He looked slightly older than her—mostly because his full head of hair was completely grey, though...hers would be, too, if she didn't dye it. They'd exchanged a bit of small talk the last few times they'd crossed paths there, but three days ago, he'd asked for her number.

She grinned just thinking about it. An attractive man had asked for her—Wendy Winslow's—number. And she'd given it to him. This afternoon, they were meeting for a late lunch at a bistro a few blocks away. She busied herself with tidying the kitchen, not because it needed to be done, but because she couldn't sit still.

Her phone buzzed on the counter.

"Mary?" she said, bringing the phone to her ear. "I thought you were out of town?"

"Because I'm out of town I can't call my friend?"

Wendy laughed. "I guess I thought you'd be too...distracted. Busy. I don't know, I didn't expect to hear from you."

"Well, I'm always glad to exceed expectations," Mary teased.

"How's Perry?" Wendy asked.

"We're going out again tomorrow night. If you remember, he was in New York for business all last week. It seems like it's been ages since I've seen him."

Wendy groaned, "Listen to yourself, Mar. You sound like a lovesick teenager. Are you doodling his name all over the palm of your hand?"

Mary laughed out loud. "That bad, is it? Sorry. I really like him."

"I got that," Wendy laughed.

"So," Mary said more soberly. "Walter's given up, then?"

"You got my text?" Wendy asked.

"I did."

"Hmm, that's odd," Wendy muttered, moving her screen in front of her and swiping to her messages. "It doesn't say you 'read' the text," she said, speaking loudly so Mary could hear her.

"Those things aren't always accurate," Mary said, her voice a soft, faraway whisper.

Wendy lifted the phone back to her ear. "It would seem so," she agreed. "Yes, if you've read that, you know the story. I'm not sure when he's going home..." she trailed off, that same pang of contrition hitting her stomach.

"Ought to be soon, I'd guess. There's no chance Walter will spend more money than he has to."

"True," Wendy scoffed. "To be fair, he did plan some date nights that were surprisingly frivolous. I honestly didn't think the man could change after so many years, but...well, who knows if he actually feels any different."

"It was an unusual circumstance," Mary agreed.

"He lost weight, Mar!" Wendy exclaimed dramatically.

"Walter?"

"Mmhmmm. He looks quite nice."

"Good for 'ol Walter," Mary laughed.

Something in Mary's tone set Wendy on edge, but she couldn't put her finger on it. She only knew she'd rather not be on the phone at the moment.

"Well, Mary, I've actually got to run."

"What do you have on?"

Wendy cleared her throat. "I'm...meeting someone. Just a friend. From the market."

"Not Cami."

"Nope."

"Gerard, by chance?"

Wendy could feel herself blushing. "It is a 'he' if that's what you're asking. His name's Paul."

"Of course it is," Mary said provocatively.

"Oh, hush," Wendy laughed. "I'll talk to you...whenever you get back."

"No, you'll call me tonight! I want to hear all about this Paul..."

Mary's exuberance softened Wendy's previous annoyance and she grinned. "I'll give you something, I promise."

"Since Perry's not available to me, I have to vicariously live through you. You have a responsibility here."

"Got it. 'Bye Mar."

She set her phone down and glanced at the clock. Still another hour before she needed to leave. Her apartment was going to be spotless.

Chapter Twenty-Six

Wendy walked determinedly along the sidewalk, her kitten heels clicking pleasantly and her wide-leg trousers flaring glamorously, just as she'd envisioned when she'd tried them on at the boutique last week. With rouge on her lips and the backdrop of charming Parisian streets, Wendy felt as if she was the leading lady in a feature film.

Her newfound freedom seemed to make her weightless. Every step she took felt positively buoyant—like she could float away on a whim. Looking across the street, she crossed as she spotted the bistro a block up on the opposite side. Taking only a few steps forward on the walkway, she halted abruptly, staring at the scene unfolding in front of her.

Halfway up the block, there was Walter. Dressed in casual trousers with a neat, button-up shirt, he looked confident and attractive. Standing in front of a cafe with an attractive woman with a grey bob, tortoiseshell glasses, and a leather purse. Though she'd noticed the change in his appearance the other night, she was now seeing him through the eyes of *that* woman, and it gave her new perspective. This wasn't the

Walter she'd come to know over the past twenty-eight years. This was someone else entirely.

She couldn't hear what they were saying, but they were engaged in intense, joyful conversation, and the woman stood with her hands stretched out, resting on Walter's arms. She leaned forward and kissed both his cheeks, then he pulled her into a warm embrace. When they parted, he gave a small wave as she walked away. Directly toward Wendy.

Thinking quickly, Wendy pulled out her phone, pretending to be looking for directions or a necessary piece of information to justify her lollygagging. The woman passed her briskly, leaving a trail of vanilla and cinnamon in her wake. Sneaking a glimpse ahead of her, she saw Walter had turned and was ambling contentedly down the street—presumably toward his flat in that direction. Wendy breathed heavily, her heart racing. Adjusting her purse, she forced herself to walk toward the bistro and find a better headspace before meeting Paul. Despite her best efforts, her thoughts were still back in the street when she pulled the door to the bistro toward her.

Back home, Wendy pulled on her joggers and opened the pint of gelato she'd emotionally purchased on her return trip to her flat. Her brunch with Paul wasn't terrible. In fact, it had gone fairly well, all things considered. He was intelligent, interesting, and spoke English with remarkable fluency and pronunciation, considering he'd never lived outside of France. Under normal circumstances, she would have described the meeting as pleasant.

Unfortunately, nothing about their date was pleasing to Wendy, because she wasn't really there. She was still frozen on the street corner replaying that woman's embrace—and kiss—with Walter over and over. When she took a sip of water, she saw it. When her food arrived at the table, it smelled of cinnamon. She smiled, nodded, and answered Paul's questions with remarkable poise and energy, all while her brain was stuck on repeat.

Plopping on the couch with a spoon in one hand and the pint in the other, she flicked on the telly. Not even bothering to change the channel, she stared at the screen and took a generous bite.

"You think he's been with her this whole time?" Mary asked, shock and disgust in her tone.

"I've no idea," Wendy said. "I'm completely flummoxed. How could he have pretended to want to solve things with me and then—and then—"

"Is he even going back home as he said?"

"I haven't spoken to him!" Wendy practically shouted. "Who knows? Maybe he said that the other night so he could move on," Wendy thought out loud, her heart pounding madly. "All this time I thought I was making the choice to break free, but perhaps—"

"No," Mary said. "You set this in motion. You made the choice. You let him go before he ever decided to—well, whatever it is he's been doing."

"You don't think—" Wendy said, her voice a whisper.

"No!" Mary exclaimed, but then hesitated. A little too long for Wendy's taste. "This should make things even easier, right?" Mary continued. "You wanted to move on, so now you can get rid of all of that responsibility and guilt I know you're feeling. He's taken action, Wendy, so there's no reason for you to sit back and worry."

"I'm not worrying—"

"We've been friends for how long?" Mary laughed. "I know you're worrying."

Wendy slipped from the chair to the floor, stretching her body out on the rug.

"It doesn't change anything," Mary insisted. "It should only make you feel better."

Wendy nodded, staring at the ceiling. "I think I'm going to head to bed," she said softly.

"Are you going to see Paul again?" she asked.

"I'm not sure…we didn't set up an exact date, but I'm sure he'll—"

"You should reach out," Mary said.

With her eyes still fixed above her, Wendy took a deep breath. "I will, thanks, Mary."

"Goodnight," she said gently. "Call anytime."

As the call ended, Wendy dropped the phone next to her, closed her eyes, and pressed her fingers to her temples.

Chapter Twenty-Seven

JANUARY, 2001

"Walt, can I speak with you a moment?" Wendy asked.

Walter held up a finger, indicating that he'd be ready in a moment. Wendy sat in the chair opposite him, glancing up at the telly where Walter's eyes were fixed. A woman dressed in primitive battle armour was racing down a grassy hill, her face fixed in fierce determination. The scene abruptly halted, interrupted by an obnoxious voice relating the benefits of a Craftmatic adjustable bed.

"Alright, what is it?" Walter asked cheerily, swiveling to face her.

Wendy took a deep breath to clear the annoyance she could already feel building in her chest. "You know the ladies from the school board?"

"Not personally—"

"You know of them," Wendy cut him off.

"Yes, I know to whom you're referring."

Wendy pursed her lips, popping them before beginning her next sentence. "We were talking this week—after dealing with a few issues, we got to chatting about what everyone does during the winter to keep from going stir-crazy—"

"Is that why those meetings run so long?" he teased.

Wendy—not even slightly in the mood—continued talking without acknowledging his comment.

"Helen mentioned that she and Janice have taken up cross-country skiing on the weekends, and I told them I'd never been."

She eyed Walter warily, inspecting his face for a reaction. When she saw nothing besides a sideways glance to the tube, she pressed on.

"Anyway, that was Janice on the phone. They're planning to head out to Boulder this weekend—they haven't yet decided on whether they'll go Saturday or Sunday—and she asked if I'd like to come along."

"You're going to go cross-country skiing?" he said with a hint of disbelief.

"I dunno, sounds like it could be fun. I've never done anything like that—"

"Do you even own any of the gear?"

"No, but I'm sure I could borrow waterproof trousers and an anorak, then I'd only need to rent skis and poles—"

"How much is this going to cost?" Walter asked with concern, turning back to the screen as the commercials came to a close.

"Janice seemed to think it would only be about thirty-five dollars for the day if I rent from a place in town," Wendy said, now staring at the side of Walter's head. "Walt?"

"If that's what you want to do..." he said dismissively.

"Well, the reason I wanted to discuss is that if we go Saturday, you'd need to take the boys to their basketball practices."

Walter didn't respond, his eyes fixed on the action ahead of him.

"If we go on Saturday," Wendy repeated, "I'd need you to take—"

"I heard you," Walter said. "I don't think that'll work, actually. I have to meet a client for lunch that day."

"Is it flexible? Could you switch it to Sunday if—"

"Couldn't you ask around and see if a friend could take them to practice?" Walter asked.

"I've already had to do that once and it's only two weeks into the season," Wendy explained.

"I can look later," Walter said, folding his hands in his lap.

Wendy stood there, her blood boiling. She could count on one hand the number of times she'd asked Walter to take over on the weekend, and never had she made a request so she could do something purely for her own recreation. She stomped into the kitchen and pulled her bar of dark chocolate from the pantry.

Chapter Twenty-Eight

JULY, 2014

"You know I'd be more than happy to stay in a hotel for the rest of this month..." Walter said for the umpteenth time.

"No," Tia responded. "That's crazy for you to be paying to live in a hotel when your house is sitting here. I really appreciate you letting me stay as long as you did," she insisted.

"But we had agreed on the full three months," he argued, "and here I am giving you two week's notice—"

"Walter, seriously. This was a gift. I had plenty of time to find other arrangements. Don't give it another thought."

Walter nodded, still feeling slightly guilty at forcing her to relocate on such short notice.

"How's Darrel doing? We haven't been able to connect for the last few weeks. He told me a little about your backpacking trip."

"Yeah, it was a blast. He's good," Tia said, smiling. "I haven't seen him much since we got back, honestly. He's been working a lot."

"It sounded like his schedule was fairly intense last time we spoke," Walter said, ignoring the tension he sensed coming from Tia. He fiddled with the gate, not sure what to say next.

"I think there might be a problem with the sprinklers," she said, walking around the side of the house and gesturing toward the head buried in the grass near the fence. The grass in that area was significantly drier than the rest of the lawn. "I was planning to work on it this week, but I didn't get a chance. I did water it by hand yesterday, so I'm hoping it'll bounce back."

"Not a problem," Walter said. "I'll look into it. Everything looks nice, thank you so much for taking such good care of it."

Tia grinned. "I tried my best."

"It shows."

"Well," Tia sighed, "I'll go get the last of my things and get out of your hair. Thanks again."

She walked back to the front of the house, and Walter heard the front door swing open and closed. He inspected the lawn and the garden, plucking a ripe cherry tomato from one of his pots. Being home made him feel as if he was observing ruins of a time past. Evidence of a life he lived, but wouldn't live again, nor would he want to. Sure, he would love to build something new with Wendy in this space, or even a different one for that matter, but he couldn't go back to what they were before. Who he was before.

He knew too much, now. He knew how his complacency had damaged the one person he thought he'd always be able to count on. More sickening than that, *he thought he'd been doing right by her*. He'd considered himself a good husband—a decent father—only to find out that every single day he'd been damaging her spirit. He couldn't let that happen again, with any of his relationships. It hurt too much.

The problem was, he didn't exactly know how to do anything differently. Other than talking to the people he cared about more and reminding himself that those people are changing all the time—he couldn't simply put them in a box like he used to. He wondered whether he had been doing this same thing to people at work unknowingly? To his children?

Staring at the tomato plant, Walter Winslow vowed to make a plan—written on paper and posted where he could see it every day—to start seeing people for who they are. Right now, at this moment. Not for who they were last year or even last week. He wanted to be curious about them, to ask more questions and actually listen to the answers. He might not be able to trust himself yet to make wide, sweeping changes in his life, but this he could do. Marching inside, noticing that Tia had already left, he plucked a pen from his old desk and a pad of paper from the drawer and began to write.

Setting his pen down and throwing the crumpled papers at his feet into the rubbage bin, Walter picked up his finished plan and pondered how and where he should post it. The wall next to the kitchen seemed like the best option since he passed it constantly. Not wanting to strip paint from the wall, he opted for two sewing pins that—for some odd reason—were in his desk drawer. Stabbing the pins through the top corners of his paper, he straightened it as best he could and pushed them into the wall.

With that task finished, he turned to haul his luggage up the stairs and begin the arduous task of unpacking. He pulled his old clothes out of the first bag and was stunned at how much larger they were. Piling them on the floor of his closet, he vowed to put them in a sack and drop them off at the donation center later in the week.

As nervous as he was to keep the new habits he'd built, he was more dedicated than ever to keep his current level of health. Those would be the next plans he'd make: a menu and exercise routine. Wendy normally made the menu, but it wasn't like cooking was completely out of his wheelhouse. He was just out of practice, that's all.

After hanging the last pair of trousers, Walter closed the suitcases and shoved them back under their bed. Wendy had picked out their bedding set and their master bedroom furniture had been a gift from his parents when they tied the knot. He wondered who would keep it, and whether he'd get to stay in this house or have to move.

The very thought of disruptions of this magnitude made him queasy. In Paris, it felt like a game. Like they were living out a dramatic fantasy with a specific endpoint. He'd been fully convinced that they'd figure it out, but now...Walter sighed, sitting lightly on the edge of the bed. This didn't have an endpoint. This was the rest of his life. Staring at a patch of blank wall, he softly sobbed.

Chapter Twenty-Nine

"Bon soir," Paul said, greeting Wendy with a kiss on the cheek.

"Bon soir," she echoed, sitting next to him on the park bench. She'd been meeting Paul at least once a week for the past month and she still felt a nervous flutter in her stomach every time he was close. He knew she wasn't officially divorced and had been a complete gentleman about it. He had divorced four years previously, which made him especially empathetic.

"Shall we?" he asked, motioning to the walking path. Wendy stood and took his arm.

"How's your week been?" Wendy asked, looking up to gauge his expression.

"Wonderful," he said, a smile spreading across his face. "I booked a trip to Bath. My art has felt stifled lately."

"Bath, sounds lovely..." Wendy said, hesitating slightly.

"What is it?" Paul asked expectantly.

"Hmm? Oh, nothing," Wendy shrugged, dropping her arm from his and opening her purse to pull out a small tin of hand salve.

"No," Paul insisted, pausing and turning her toward him. "What is it about Bath—"

"It's really nothing," Wendy said. "I was just surprised, that's all. Last time we spoke, you talked about how your sales hadn't been what you'd expected and finances were tight, so—"

Paul sighed heavily, pulling her along as he began walking forward again. "You don't understand, Wendy. And I can't blame you. As an artist, I have to be inspired, regardless of the cost. Sometimes my finances are up and that feels great," he laughed, nudging her, "but most of the time, I'm on the edge."

"Isn't that stressful?" she asked honestly.

"It is, but it's useful risk—constant volatility helps me create my best work. My most meaningful pieces have come weeks or even days before I thought I was being evicted."

"That's happened more than once?"

"Happens all the time!" he said, laughing heartily. He reached out and tapped her nose affectionately. "My Wendy. So naive to the dark side of being a dreamer."

"Not that naive," she pouted.

Paul put his arm around her shoulder. "You'll see it all eventually. But the ups far exceed the downs once you get used to it."

Wendy forced a smile and quickly changed the subject.

Back at her flat, she stripped off her clothes and hopped into the shower. It had been surprisingly warm today, and she'd sweated right through her deodorant. Tossing her clothes in the dirty bin, she turned on the water and pulled the curtain around her, hitting the toilet and sink with water before she was able to tilt the shower head in the correct direction. She still hadn't gotten used to the feeling of a plastic curtain clinging to her wet skin as she washed her hair. Though her shower wasn't anything special back in Colorado, she found herself thinking of it wistfully in moments like this.

Her conversation with Paul in the park percolated as she squeezed conditioner into her palm. Surely there had to be a way to live one's dreams without regularly missing your rent payment. His life didn't sound exactly 'free' to her. From what she could gather, he was constantly worried about where the next check would be coming from and whether it would get to him on-time.

She had to admit, some of his darkest pieces were her favorite. His *Midnight Ink* oil on canvas abstract was breathtaking, but if she was honest, also somewhat disturbing. Perhaps for his dreams, he really *did* need the juxtaposition of highs and lows, light and dark, to drag his brooding creativity to the forefront. But Wendy's dreams were simpler. She could still be a dreamer without the turmoil and angst, couldn't she?

Turning off the water, she opened the curtain and pulled a towel from the small shelf next to the door. She dried herself, then wrapped the towel around her and walked to her bedroom for clean clothes. As she reached for a clean shirt, her phone buzzed on the counter, startling her. The towel she'd been holding dropped to the floor and—though she knew nobody could see her—she hastily plucked it off the rug and wrapped it snugly around her torso before tiptoeing across the floor to glance at the screen.

"Mary," she said warmly, holding the phone to her ear. "How—"

"It's over, Wendy," Mary sobbed. "Perry and me."

"No, I gathered it was Perry you were talking about," Wendy said, moving to the chair and sitting down. "I'm so sorry, Mar. What happened? It sounded like things were going so well."

"They were!" she sniffed. "At least, *I* thought they were. We haven't even had a proper conversation about it, he just stopped calling me back. One minute he's putting forth effort and telling me I'm a breath of fresh air, and the next? Radio silence. I don't know what I did wrong..."

"Mary, stop. I doubt it was anything you did—"

"Wouldn't it have to be? If it was him, wouldn't he have had the decency to explain?"

"That's the thing. Most people when they're in the midst of struggle don't really have the skills to communicate properly. Hence the reason we all get hurt. I don't think anyone *means* to hurt another, it just...happens, because we're not at our best."

"He seemed fine when we were together last," Mary argued, blowing her nose in what Wendy hoped was a tissue.

"I'm so sorry," Wendy repeated.

"Here I am, mid-fifties and I'm *alone*, Wendy. And I'm not like you. You've still got a figure and a pretty face," Mary spluttered. "My hair is thinning by the day, the skin under my eyes looks like a bloated frog's vocal sack, and—"

"Alright, Mar, that's absolutely enough!" Wendy said firmly. "I know you're gutted right now, but I'm not going to listen to that rubbish. We're both getting older, it's true, but we have a lot to offer, and it might just take some time before we find—"

"But what if I never do!?" Mary cut in. "I'll be an old spinster with knitting needles in every size and seven cats. That's not exactly how I envisioned my life."

Wendy laughed, "That won't happen. You hate cats."

"That's how desperate the situation is!" Mary moaned. "I'm considering sharing my life with abnormally small, narcissistic mammals rather than face the next thirty years of my life pathetically eating breakfast alone."

Sighing, Wendy stood and walked back to the kitchen for a glass of water. Cradling the phone against her shoulder, she took a sip. "Mary, you're not going to be alone for the rest of your life," Wendy said gently.

"But what if I am?" she said with heartbreaking sincerity. "This whole thing is harder than I thought."

"I'm so sorry, Mar."

"It's alright," she said. "I didn't mean to be a wet blanket. What have you been up to?" she asked.

Wendy hesitated. "Nothing much, sight-seeing. I actually just got out of the shower, so I should probably put on some clothes."

"We just had this entire conversation while you were nude?" Mary laughed.

"I've got a towel on, for goodness' sake."

"Fine then, get dressed. I've got some errands to run over the next couple of days, but let's talk end of the week?"

"Sounds great," Wendy said. Setting the phone down, she leaned against the counter and scanned her living space. Everything was exactly how she left it—nothing out of place. She picked up her clothes and stalked to the bathroom to hang up her towel and get dressed for the second time that day.

Chapter Thirty

"Welcome back," Ted said, reaching out and firmly shaking Walter's hand. "We've taken good care of the place."

"I can see that," Walter nodded.

"What brought you back early? I hope the trip went well—?"

"Oh yes, everything was lovely. It was...just a long time to be gone," Walter said, pursing his lips.

"I can see that. We're definitely glad to have you back."

Ted retreated to his office—one of only four in the small rental space. Over the years, Walter had grown his accounting firm from a desk in his own living room to a single office to this: half a floor of a three-story building in a plaza sharing a parking lot with Whole Foods. He employed three other CPA's and two front-desk staff, and up until this very moment, he'd been incredibly proud of his business. He loved the consistency of numbers and the fact that even the most mismanaged accounts could be put back into order with enough digging and attention to detail. It hadn't been easy for him to take the risk of hiring employees and actively working to build his clientele, but he had been somewhat successful at it. Now, looking around at the white walls, cheap blinds, and industrial carpet, this office felt more like a juvenile prison.

His career hadn't been for him, not really. He'd chosen something that made sense because his ultimate goal was to provide for his family. To provide for Wendy. Now that there was nobody to provide for...what was the point?

Walter walked into his office to find a large pile of paperwork with multicolored sticky notes protruding from between the crisp, white edges. He recognized it would have been too much to ask for Ted to have completely taken over his accounts, but he still wasn't looking forward to dealing with eight weeks worth of problem cases. At least it wasn't the first quarter. Plenty of time to catch up. He stared at his chair behind the desk, then turned and walked out into the common area to get a cup of water.

"Right after work?" Jill asked, standing in the doorway to Stephanie's office.

"Yeah, as soon as everyone can finish up," Walter heard Stephanie answer.

"How old is he turning?"

Walter couldn't hear the response this time, but Jill laughed.

"Sounds great," Jill said, turning and striding toward the copier.

"What's right after work?" Walter asked nonchalantly as he passed her on his way to his office.

"Oh," she said, glancing around the office, "a few of us are going to take Ted out for his birthday after work. He doesn't know yet," she said, winking conspiratorially.

Walter cleared his throat. "Would it...be alright if I joined you?"

Jill looked startled. "Of course, that would be great. Normally when we've planned things you've been—"

"Busy," Walter finished her sentence. "Or just anti-social," he said with a wan smile.

Jill laughed.

"Wendy's still overseas, so I'm quite un-busy and surprisingly, not feeling anti-social," he said, his cheeks flushing.

"Well we'd love to have you come," she said sincerely.

Walter nodded. "See you then."

Jill smiled, continuing on her path to make copies.

Walter arrived home at eight twenty-five that night to find Darrel's car parked in the driveway. Concerned, he quickly walked through the front door to find his son seated in the living room.

"That's a tad eerie, don't you think?" Walter said, turning on the light.

"Good to see you, too, Dad," Darrel said, looking up from his phone.

"You're going to damage your eyesight staring at a bright screen like that in the pitch dark."

"Luckily, this isn't a habit of mine," Darrel retorted with a smile.

"Just when you want to give your ol' Dad a fright," Walter muttered, setting his bag next to the coat rack, slipping off his shoes, and walking into the kitchen.

"Did I really scare you?" Darrel laughed.

Walter grunted.

"And what were you doing out so late?" Darrel asked, following him out of the room and sitting down at the kitchen table. "I've been waiting here for almost two hours. I was about to call the police."

"You could've just phoned me," Walter said, pulling a glass from the cupboard and filling it with water from the tap.

"It's a figure of speech, Dad," Darrel said, rolling his eyes. "But seriously, why're you home so late?"

Walter sighed, sitting down next to his son and taking a gulp. "I went out for Ted's birthday."

"Who's Ted?"

"What d'you mean 'Who's Ted'? Ted's worked with me at the office for nearly half your life!"

"Ah, that Ted. Sorry, I didn't really think you two were...friends."

"Well, we're not—we work well together, but—" Walter spluttered, attempting to explain.

"It doesn't matter," Darrel said gently, "I'm just surprised, that's all. You always used to arrive home at the exact same time, so it was a shock to find you not home."

Walter nodded, taking another drink. "I suppose so," he said. "I'm still usually home at the same time, it's just...the staff were going out and...I didn't exactly relish the idea of coming back to an empty house."

Darrel leaned back in his chair. "Dad," he said, taking a deep breath. "What's going on?"

"What do you mean?" Walter asked, feigning ignorance.

"Well, for starters, what happened to your moustache?"

Walter laughed out loud, nearly spilling his glass of water. The question took him so off-guard that it took him approximately three whole minutes to compose himself. Wiping a tear from his eye, he looked at his son squarely.

"It was time for a change," he said soberly.

Darrel nodded, the grin disappearing from his face. "Was Mum wanting a change, as well?" he asked softly.

Walter looked down at the table, tapping his glass with his index finger. He nodded.

"So it wasn't a holiday. This whole trip to Paris."

"No," Walter breathed. "That was me—" his voice caught

in his throat and he took another drink. “That was me,” he started again, “attempting to fix things.”

“Did it work?” Darrel asked hopefully.

Walter gestured around him at the empty house. “I did my very best, son.”

“Obviously not good enough,” Darrel said under his breath, then looked up apologetically. “Sorry, I didn’t mean that.”

“No, it’s fine,” Walter said, not meeting his eyes. “It was too little too late.”

“What does that mean?” Darrel asked, his voice carrying a tinge of annoyance. “Is Mum just living in Paris now? She’s not even going to come back to explain this to us herself?”

Walter put a hand on his shoulder. “It’s all fairly fresh. I don’t think she has any intention of staying in Paris, and—besides that—your mum’s a good woman. She’s not going to leave you hanging. I think she’s sorting things out and when she’s ready, she’ll explain.”

Darrel ran his hands through his hair, pain and confusion evident on his face.

“Tia made it sound like your schedule is unforgiving at the moment,” Walter said, attempting to change the subject.

“That’s an understatement,” Darrel quipped.

“How is it that you had time to drive all the way up here tonight?”

“I didn’t exactly have time, but I wanted to see you. When I heard Mum hadn’t come back with you—” he paused, looking down at his hands. “I was worried about you. And worried about Mum.”

“Darrel, that’s very kind of you, but we’re going to be alright. If you have work you need to do, don’t let your dear old dad keep you from it,” Walter said, standing and setting his glass next to the sink.

“Can I stay here tonight?” Darrel asked. “I’ll need to leave early to get back in time for class, but...it's late. And I'm exhausted—"

"You don't need to justify it to me, Darrel. Of course you can stay," Walter said, his heart swelling at the thought of not sleeping alone for the first time in months.

"Thanks," Darrel said.

"I can't promise everything is clean and tidy the way your mother has things when you come to visit. Though I haven't had much time to really mess things up."

"I'm not worried about it," Darrel chuckled.

"Well," Walter said, walking toward the stairs. When he reached the first step, he turned toward his youngest son. "See you in the morning."

"Goodnight," Darrel nodded.

Chapter Thirty-One

"Ha! There you are," Wendy said, spotting Cami amidst the other tourists just down the hill from her. Slipping her phone back into her purse, she strode toward her, the afternoon sun warm against her skin.

"I didn't realize you were up by the church," Cami said as soon as Wendy was within earshot.

"I should've been more specific with my directions," Wendy laughed. "Though, this is my first time here. I didn't quite know what to expect."

"Mine, too," Cami said. "Doesn't matter! We connected and now I think it's time to go see this gorgeous church."

"Agreed," Wendy said, glancing up at the impressive facade. The domes of the Sacre Coeur Basilica were understandably more striking up close than from a distance. Though she and Walter had passed by the Moulin Rouge and other historical sites below, they hadn't made the trek up. When Cami mentioned she'd been wanting to walk through the artists square, they decided to make a day of it.

"It's not overwhelmingly busy," Wendy noted. "I'm glad we came on a weekday."

"Me, too," Cami agreed. "I'm sorry I haven't been available to do our dinners the past few weeks."

"I know you've been busy—that's a good thing, isn't it?"

Cami nodded. "It really is. My classes are fantastic, and I've met some really incredible people. I do miss our chats, though."

"Ah," Wendy waved her off. "I doubt that anything I have to say is more interesting than the things you're hearing from the most enlightened people in Paris," she teased.

Cami rolled her eyes. "I wouldn't go that far."

They hushed their voices and Wendy removed her sunhat as they entered the church. The air inside seemed to settle on them—still, yet rich with history and the palpable feel of silent meditation. Wendy's eyes were immediately drawn up to the brilliantly colored stained glass windows. The sunlight danced through the individual panes leaving kaleidoscopic patterns on the marble. She noticed each patron saint as they made their pilgrimage to the center of the church.

Though she hadn't ever been particularly religious, Wendy made the snap decision to sit and meditate in one of the pews. She looked around nervously, wondering if she was allowed to sit. When no security guards immediately appeared, she breathed a sigh of relief. Feeling somewhat silly and out of practice, she gazed up at the depiction of the Savior high above her. The inlay gold and intricate details took her breath away.

Closing her eyes, she inhaled deeply. Not knowing whether there was a God to hear her, she began to silently pour out her soul. She'd seen this trip in her mind for years—not necessarily what she'd do, but *who she'd be*. Free. Finding new purpose. Soaking in new adventures. Anger welled up inside her as she thought this. Technically, she was outwardly doing everything she always thought she would, but she'd fought for weeks to shove down the incessantly gnawing realization that she didn't feel free. Every emotion—every thought

—was tied to her previous relationships. She couldn't experience anything without first filtering it through Calvin's eyes, or Darrel's, or—as much as she hated to admit it—Walter's.

Why couldn't she cut the strings and be done with it? Not with her children, of course, but with the responsibility she felt to make all of them approve. They were grown men, and it wasn't in her job description to only be a mother the rest of her life. Yet she thought almost daily about what they'd think if they knew she'd met with Paul…or that he kissed her.

Why did she care so much about their opinions? The anger simmering within her seemed to flare as she thought of Walter. He had done this! He'd made her feel like the bad guy. He'd planted seeds of doubt with all his talk about 'people not being happy' after they'd gotten a divorce. He'd made her feel guilty by trying so hard and suddenly being willing to try when all these years—

Wendy squeezed her eyes tightly as tears begin to well up and spill over onto her cheeks. Why couldn't he have been willing years ago? She didn't love Paul, she knew that. He was obsessed with his art and—though she hated that she was thinking it—a little practicality and realistic organization would do him good.

Her heart started to beat faster and her chest felt tight. What if she'd been wrong? About Walter, about herself. What if she'd done all of this only to find out that this life of dreaming—of whimsy—that seemed so attractive to her wasn't what she actually wanted? Even worse, what if she didn't know what she wanted? How could she have lived this long and not even known what would actually make her happy? *What if she'd never be happy?*

This last thought slammed into her, knocking the breath out of her lungs. She leaned forward, resting her head on her arms as they rested on the back of the pew in front of her. She didn't know what she was doing, and she didn't know where to turn for help. Her tears flowed freely as she offered a silent prayer to the heavens.

A few moments later, Wendy felt a gentle tap on her shoulder. Her body jerked upright and she scrambled to wipe the tears from her cheeks.

"It's just me," Cami said gently. "Thought I should check in with you."

Wendy looked up at her with red-rimmed eyes, then scooted over on the bench allowing her to sit down. Cami reached her arm around Wendy's shoulder and squeezed.

"You doing okay?" Cami asked.

Not trusting herself to speak yet, Wendy motioned to her puffy face.

Cami laughed. "Well, right, I see that you're upset, I just didn't know if this was 'I'm overwhelmed with the beauty all around me' or 'I'm a terrible person and I've disappointed God,'" Cami said dramatically, and Wendy looked at her quizzically.

"That's how I always feel when I walk into churches," Cami said, quickly looking down at her feet.

"You feel like a terrible person?" Wendy asked gently, pulling a tissue from her purse and blowing her nose.

Cami nodded hesitantly. "Kind of? I was raised Catholic and since I left the house, I haven't been to mass more than a handful of times. And that was usually because someone else invited me to go along with them. I definitely don't live in a way my parents would approve of."

"That doesn't mean you're a terrible person," Wendy said, shaking her head.

"Maybe not. I still feel like I'm letting Him down or something," she sighed, gazing at the vignettes above. "Like him, for example," she said, pointing at the statue to their right. "*He* gave up his riches—everything he had—to follow Him. And I'm not even willing to give up a Sunday picnic."

Wendy laughed out loud and quickly covered her mouth with her hand.

"Oh darling, you're being a little too hard on yourself, I think. That's why we come to churches, eh?" Wendy said quietly. "So we can be inspired." She nudged Cami's shoulder.

Cami grinned, her eyes shimmering with tears.

"We all have different paths," Wendy said, looking past the altar. "I don't know if He's there, Cami. I honestly don't. But I know we'll all find our way eventually. What other choice do we have?"

She looked at Cami a moment, then slumped over, exhaling loudly. "But don't listen to me, dear. Truth is, I'm second guessing all the choices I've made over the last year. And the years before that. I've no clue what I'm doing...and, I think...I might be more selfish than I thought. And I may have ruined everything—" she said, her voice breaking.

"I'm sorry," Cami whispered, not sure what she could say to console her friend. "I think it might be okay to be a little lost, right? To feel wrong sometimes. Even our poor choices teach us something, I think. Sometimes even more than our good ones."

Wendy raised an eyebrow. "That's a fair bit of wisdom coming from a young thing like yourself. You might need to take your own advice," she teased.

An usher walked past their pew motioning for them to be quieter. Wendy nodded apologetically.

"Should we take this outside, or do you need a few more moments?" Cami whispered.

Wendy nodded, then mouthed, "Let's go" as she stood up. Outside, Cami excitedly began walking down the street toward the artists with their artwork and easels strewn across the walkways lining the street. Wendy followed, her breathing finally back to normal and her body feeling lighter than it had all week. What was that emotional outburst in there? And what was she supposed to learn from this, exactly? It seemed that any choice she made carried consequences she couldn't anticipate—or even if she could, she wasn't sure she was ready to face them.

Again, the fear of perpetually seeking, yet never finding clawed at her heart. She buried it deep as she passed painting after painting, distracting herself with the brushstrokes and swirls of color. She knew these feelings wouldn't stay hidden forever, but for now, she focused on the joy on Cami's face and the whimsy and creativity on the streets of Montmartre.

Chapter Thirty-Two

AUGUST, 2014

"Are you coming along tonight?" Jill asked, poking her head into Walter's office.

"Don't tell me I've forgotten another birthday," Walter said with a wry grin.

"Nope, just a regular 'drinks after work' thing," she said.

"As long as I can get through these accounts—"

Jill waved him off. "Those accounts can wait."

"You only say that because you're not the one writing the paychecks," Walter chuckled.

"Just trying to help with your work-life balance," she teased, walking back to her office.

Walter shook his head with a smile, returning his focus to his monitor. Over the past couple of weeks, the office had been...different. Since he thrived on consistency, he'd never struggled with boredom or the repetitive nature of his work, but he'd also never felt particularly excited about it. Every day simply was. He'd never expected anything beyond that, and therefore, he wasn't ever disappointed. But, now that he was spending time with those he worked with, he felt an extra spring in his step. He even found himself leaving home at closer to ten-past seven. Five minutes earlier than necessary.

He reached across his desk and pulled a manila folder from the stack, searching for a client's Schedule K from the past year. Finding it immediately, he copied the numbers onto a sticky note. Rolling his chair away from the desk, he took a moment to flex his feet and stretch his calves. Though he hadn't been able to find a way to realistically run to work without waking up painfully early, he had tried biking one morning. When he arrived at the office drenched in sweat, he briefly considered taking a paper-towel sponge bath in the WC, but thankfully recognized the absurdity of that thought before he found himself in a compromising position.

Yet, he hadn't given up on keeping the positive fitness habits he'd built in France. Each night, the words "keep promises to myself" stared back at him from his list posted on the wall. Which meant that every night, he laid out his running clothes and set his alarm forty minutes earlier than usual.

Sorrow washed over his face as he abruptly reached for his water and took a drink. Thinking about his morning routine always revived memories of his life with Wendy. His running routine, as enlivening as it was, didn't fill the void he felt each time he dressed and cooked his breakfast in solitude.

Walter's phone rang, startling him. Without looking at the caller ID, he picked it up.

"Winslow Accounting, this is Walter."

"Dad," Calvin exhaled, his voice distraught.

"Cal? Are you alright?" he said, immediately alert.

His son was silent on the other end.

"Calvin? Are you—"

Calvin gasped for breath. "I'm here," he choked out.

"What is going on?" Walter asked, becoming more

concerned by the second. He'd seen his son cry exactly twice in his adult life. Once at his wedding and once when he stubbed his toe severely on the edge of a picnic table.

"Dad," Calvin repeated. "We lost the baby," he sobbed.

"What?" Walter asked, not able to process the words he was hearing.

"Becky. She miscarried. They just took her back for surgery—I'm here by myself, there's nothing—" He continued on, but his words were unintelligible.

"Calvin," Walter cut in. "What hospital are you at?"

He scribbled down the information, shoved the sticky note in his pocket, and turned off his computer. Explaining to Jill hastily as he left his office, he ran to his car and immediately dialed Southwest Airlines.

Wendy stood next to Paul on Rue Saint-Maur. They'd walked nearly one kilometer already and her feet were sore.

"Do you see how Kashink uses these lines to enhance the femininity of her work?" Paul said, completely in awe.

Wendy stared at the four eyes peering back at her, the colors so bright she was tempted to shield her eyes. It looked like a child's drawing. A very disturbed child, at that.

"It's intriguing," she said, attempting to deepen her artistic understanding, but coming up short.

"She's just so...brave!" Paul continued. "Her willingness to play with cultural norms and stereotypes," he sighed. "Such an inspiration."

Wendy squinted her eyes, willing herself to find meaning in the pink, jelly-bean shaped head with a moustache. Her phone vibrated in her pocket providing a much-needed distraction. Pulling it out, her eyes widened and she stood stock-still with her hand still extended in the air.

"Aren't you going to answer it?" Paul asked, vaguely aware

of her hesitation, but not able to tear his eyes from the wall in front of him.

Wendy tentatively touched the screen, then raised the phone to her ear.

"Walter?" she questioned.

"Wendy," he said, out of breath. "I'm so glad we've finally gotten a hold of you."

"What are you talking about? I haven't seen any calls come through—"

"I'm not sure what the problem was," Walter cut in, "but Calvin's been trying to call you all evening."

"What time is it there..." she said under her breath, flipping over her wrist to check her watch. "Walter," she said, her voice thick with concern. "It's one in the morning in Colorado. What's going on?"

"Well, technically, it's only midnight here. I'm in California."

"What!?" she exclaimed, her concern and confusion showing plainly on her face and in her tone.

"Is everything alright?" Paul asked, moving closer, but Wendy quickly shushed him.

"Go on, Walter," Wendy said hurriedly.

"Who's that?" Walter asked.

"It doesn't matter!" Wendy said firmly. "For goodness' sake, Walter, spit it out!"

Walter exhaled loudly. "I'm about to go into the hospital—" he started, but before he could get the next words out, Wendy collapsed to the pavement, the blood draining from her face. Paul—finally recognizing the intensity of the situation—crouched next to her and placed a hand on her back.

"Please, Walter, tell me Calvin's safe—"

"He's safe," Walter promised. "But Wendy. They lost the baby."

Wendy's mouth moved, but no words came out. Her eyes locked on the rubbish bin directly in front of her face.

"Wendy?" Walter said gently. "Wendy, I'm sorry, I've got to get in there. Becky's gone back and Calvin's all alone—"

"Which hospital?" she said, her voice robotic.

"Wendy, dear, nobody expects you—"

"*Which hospital!*" she shrieked, squeezing the phone so tightly that her fingers began to go numb.

"I'll send you a message," Walter said quickly. Then, pausing, his voice seemed to float in the air—crossing the Atlantic and piercing her heart. "I'm so sorry, Wendy."

The call ended and, though Wendy was vaguely aware of Paul's concerned voice behind her, the ringing in her ears was too all-encompassing to pick out the words he was saying. She clutched the phone to her chest, suddenly riveted by the one-dimensional, flamboyant character on the bricks in front of her. The grotesque face seemed to be sneering at her—laughing at her dashed hope that she would have the privilege of holding her son's tiny baby in her arms.

"Should we move on to the next?" Paul asked hesitantly, his voice finally breaking through her mental fog.

Wendy's head snapped his direction. Having forgotten he was there for a moment, it took her time to recover and answer appropriately.

"No, Paul," she said, clearing her throat and carefully lifting herself from the pavement. "I don't think we'll be moving on to anything."

When she arrived at the airport a few hours later, she was numb. Everything was a blur. Honestly, she couldn't even remember what she'd done after she left Paul. If she hadn't been currently pulling her suitcase along the tile floor, she might have doubted whether she'd gone home to pack it or not.

The news from Walter was still sinking in. Slowly, the reality of losing a grandchild before she even had one was absorbing into her being, layer after agonizing layer. *How could Becky have lost this baby?* Everything had been normal, and they were far beyond the safety milestone of twelve weeks.

Guilt ate at her for not calling them more or being involved at all in the pregnancy. Maybe if she'd been more involved she could've helped them recognize the problem before it became life-threatening. Even as her thoughts spiraled into this wormhole of regret, she knew it was pointless. All the 'should haves' or 'could haves' in the world likely wouldn't have been enough to change anything. And how ridiculous was it for her to think she would've known anything better than her son and daughter-in-law?

As she boarded the plane, her body jittered with nervous energy. She waited impatiently as passengers in front of her slowly made their way through the tunnel to the aircraft. Stepping aboard, she smiled politely at a flight attendant with long blonde hair that was pulled up into an oppressively high ponytail. She found her row and sidled into the window seat, grateful that she wouldn't have to stand up to accommodate the bathroom needs of the individuals in her row. Turning her back to everyone, she lifted the window shade and stared into the inky night.

Chapter Thirty-Three

A knock on the door pulled Calvin from his recliner. Looking through the peephole of his townhome, he quickly reached for the door handle. Wendy nearly toppled him with an embrace as soon as the door swung open. Calvin stumbled backward, but kept a strong grip on his mother and was somehow able to remain upright.

"Calvin, I'm so sorry," she said, her voice muffled by the collar of his shirt.

"You didn't have to—"

"I had to," she said, cutting him off.

They held each other for a few moments, then Wendy stepped back, turned toward the open door, and pulled her small suitcase in from the step.

"I had to talk myself down when I heard they'd already sent her home," Wendy said, her eyes flashing as she took a seat in the chair opposite the men. She hadn't yet acknowledged Walter's presence and that fact didn't escape Calvin's notice.

"She's resting," Calvin said, exhaling audibly as he sat down again. He ran his hands over his face, blinking his bloodshot eyes.

"How did the surgery go?" Wendy asked.

"As well as could be expected. It was intense because she was so far along," he said, his voice breaking. Squeezing his eyes shut, he leaned back in the chair, attempting to compose himself.

Wendy's eyes immediately filled with tears as she watched her son breaking. Never in her life had she seen him like this. Calvin was always in control. As an oldest child, his confidence was frightening to her at times, especially when it was in such complete juxtaposition to her own insecurities.

Seeing him like this—defeated and harrowed up with grief—left her feeling like the ground was shifting beneath her. And her ground wasn't steady to begin with.

"I don't know how to help," Walter said. "Could I go to the store? Get us food for breakfast?"

"Are you staying here?" Wendy asked, her voice formal and overly polite.

"I stayed last night," Walter said, "but I'm happy t0—"

"No," Calvin said abruptly. "I don't know what is going on with you two, but I'm not doing this."

"Doing what?" Wendy asked innocently.

"Did you talk to Darrel?" Walter asked at the same moment.

"Darrel? What would Darrel have to say—" Wendy started.

"Stop! I'm not doing—whatever *this* is," Calvin said, gesturing to both of them. "The tension is so thick I could cut it with a knife, and I just lost my son—" he said, sucking in a ragged breath. "I'm so grateful you both came to support me, but I can't handle anything else. I need you to just be my parents right now."

Walter nodded and Wendy pursed her lips. Calvin stood, ran his hands through his hair, and looked around the room as if searching for an explanation of the last twenty-four hours;

one that could take away the hole in his chest and the pit in his stomach. Without saying another word, he stalked out of the room.

Wendy looked at the floor, her posture strained.

"I can get a hotel room for the night," Walter said softly.

"That's clearly not what Calvin wants," Wendy snapped, regretting her tone immediately. She hadn't meant to take anything out on Walter, but also wasn't in a state to apologize.

"I know," Walter agreed, his voice surprisingly calm, "but I'm too old to sleep on the floor," he said with a self-deprecating laugh.

"We're both adults," Wendy said, brushing off her trousers. "I think we can handle spending one night together for the sake of our son."

Walter nodded, still not able to meet her eyes. The last time he'd seen her had been in that art museum. It felt like ages ago. She hadn't called or tried to contact him at all, and this had been more hurtful than he'd be willing to admit. Some part of him had believed and hoped that walking away would ignite something in her. Help her to realize that some part of her might still care for him.

"We're both adults," Walter repeated softly. "And yet our son is dictating our sleeping arrangements."

Wendy rolled her eyes. "You can't blame him, given the current circumstances." She exhaled loudly, raising her hand to massage the back of her neck. "It's a lot," she whispered.

Walter nodded in agreement, noticing how Wendy's eyes shimmered with tears. He stood and walked toward her—his hands aching to wipe away her tears—then leaned down and wrapped them around the handle of her overnight bag instead.

"Thank you," Wendy said, watching Walter take her things to the guest room.

. . .

Wendy hesitantly stepped into the room after washing her face and brushing her teeth in the bathroom across the hall. Walter was already in bed and her heart squeezed at the scene before her. Walter was propped up on the left side of the mattress with his bottom half under the blankets reading a book, his glasses hanging precariously on the tip of his nose. The familiarity of this scene was unexpectedly and overwhelmingly comforting. She quickly looked away and tucked her toiletry bag into her suitcase.

Eventually, running out of distracting organizational tasks, she turned to the bed.

"I can sleep on top of the sheets," Walter suggested.

"You would hate that," Wendy muttered.

And Walter erupted. "Alright, I've had just about enough of this nonsense," he said, slamming his book closed and dropping it to his lap, then pushing his glasses up so he could finally look at her. "Why is it that you have permission to tell me everything *I* like. That *I want*, but the second I make assumptions about you, I'm 'putting you in a box'?"

Wendy stood stiffly next to the bed, her eyes wide. Walter had never spoken to her like this. Or anyone, for that matter. Well, except when the children were misbehaving, but that was years ago...and she had much appreciated it at the time.

"I'm not sure what you mean..." she hedged, her heart hammering in her chest.

"Is that or is that not your main criticism of our marriage? That I put you in a box and expect you to be the same year after year? I haven't put in effort to get to know you, and I don't give you room to change and—and follow your dreams?" Walter spluttered, repeating word-for-word the explanations he'd heard from her over the past months.

"No, you're not listening," she said in a patronizing tone. "You *like* everyone to fit in a box. That's what makes you comfortable. When life is predictable and people act in practical, rational ways—"

"Aha!" Walter said, pointing his finger in accusation. "Don't you see? That's *you putting me in a box.* Telling me what I like and what makes me comfortable! You won't let *me* grow either! You think I don't like change, but what if I've simply never had the opportunity or the motivation to learn to be okay with it? I know it's difficult for you to believe, but I enjoyed Paris."

Wendy raised an eyebrow.

"Sure," he conceded, "I was uncomfortable and it was painful for me at times, but it honestly opened my eyes in so many important ways. I'm not the same man I was two months ago, Wendy, and you won't let me be different. You won't let me make a new choice or surprise you because you jump in with all of these assumptions and make the decision for me," he finished, his face flushed.

Wendy scowled. "That's not what I'm doing," she said, her voice low.

"It's exactly what you're doing, but it's easier for you to put all the blame on me as if I'm the only one that has responsibility—"

"Walter stop!" she hissed, not wanting to alert Calvin or Becky to their disagreement. "I can't take any more tonight. My son and his wife lost their first child, and I—" she said, her voice breaking. "Was thrilled—selfishly perhaps—to be a grandma, and *I'm not a grandma anymore...*" she said, trailing off and squeezing her eyes closed as her hand flew to cover her mouth.

"Wendy...I'm sorry, I didn't think—" Walter started compassionately, only to be cut off by Wendy's palm held up in his direction. Not wanting to make things worse, Walter snapped his mouth shut. He picked up his book, but quickly realized he wasn't capable of concentrating on the words on the page. Setting it on the nightstand, he placed his spectacles on top of the book and turned off the light.

Walter watched his wife of twenty-eight years quietly slip into bed with her back coldly and purposefully turned to him. By the way her shoulders gently shook, he could tell she was crying. Too anxious to reach out to her, he shifted in the bed, hoping to remind her that he was there should she need him.

Then, realizing his words were the catalyst—if not the entire cause—for her emotional distress, he began to mentally berate himself for his insensitivity, as he had so many times over the last few months. This time, however, he caught himself. His timing hadn't been right, but his point was valid. For the first time, he was positive that this whole mess wasn't entirely his fault. As Wendy's breathing came in bursts next to him, tears leaked from the corners of his eyes and streaked down his cheek, wrapping behind his ears and dampening his pillow.

Chapter Thirty-Four

JULY, 1999

"I know it's summer, but it might be a bit chilly at the park this early in the day," Wendy said, holding out a light jacket to Calvin who crossed his arms over his chest and set his jaw.

"I don't want to wear a coat, Mum," he said. His growth over the last year had been astonishing to Walter and Wendy, and the new angles appearing on his face spoke to a loss of childhood they weren't ready to confront.

"Let the boy make his choice," Walter said, descending the stairs to the landing. "I can carry the jacket just in case."

Wendy sighed, her frustration evident.

"I've got a jumper on!" Darrel announced excitedly. "I don't want to be cold."

"Good on you," Wendy said, praising him as Calvin rolled his eyes. "Let's be off, then," she said.

The Winslow family stepped out the door and began to walk down the street. The boys ran slightly ahead as they tagged each other, then dodged to escape the other's grasp.

Wendy smiled at their playfulness as Walter slipped his hand in hers.

"They're good boys," Walter said.

"They are," Wendy agreed.

"What do you think the next ten years of our lives will look like?" he asked, and Wendy took a moment to ponder this.

"I've no idea," she answered honestly. "I'm still recovering from the toddler years, I can't think that far ahead," she laughed.

"It's hard to imagine them as young men," Walter said. "I think it'll come faster than we think."

Wendy nodded. "It's already moving too fast," she said, then raised her voice, reminding the boys to wait at the edge of the street before crossing. They walked faster to catch up and took each boy by the hand, walking across to the next block.

Catching view of the park, the boys took off down the path with exuberance.

"Oh to be young again," Walter said.

Wendy smiled, her hand still warmed by Walter's as they walked.

"I don't really have an identity outside of them," she said softly. "All of the activities I loved growing up—I haven't explored any of them since having children."

"That's normal, isn't it?" Walter said. "And, if you remember, you were the one who wanted to start a family young," he teased.

"I know," Wendy said, "and I haven't regretted it. But thinking about the future makes me...I don't know, a little nervous? I wonder if I've lost myself a bit."

"You seem like the same Wendy to me," Walter said, attempting to buoy up her spirits.

"You're probably right," she said, pulling him to a bench.

As they sat, Wendy watched the boys jump and play, finding sticks and using them to swirl the water of the pond.

"Is this what life is?" she asked. "Growing up and having babies so they can grow up and have babies?"

"When you say it like that, it sounds a little grim," Walter chuckled.

"I don't mean it to be," Wendy said, "I've just been thinking. What's the point of it all? Why do we work so hard to do the same thing day after day?"

Walter turned to her, inspecting her face. "Are you alright, love?"

"Of course," she said, taking a deep breath.

"Are you unhappy with your life?" Walter asked sincerely.

"No, not at all. I think it's just...different than I anticipated. When I was a child, I thought being an adult would be magical," she laughed, looking down at her hands.

"Isn't it, though?" Walter asked, pointing at their children talking to a girl their age under a tree.

"A different kind of magical," she admitted.

"In ten years, I think Calvin will be attending Oxford and Darrel," Walter stopped short, musing. "Darrel could be an entrepreneur of some sort."

"What makes you think that?" Wendy asked, amused.

"He's creative," Walter shrugged.

"He'd still need an education," Wendy said.

"Definitely," Walter agreed. "I don't actually have a clue about them," he laughed, "but I think you and I...we could buy a house in the country and escape there on the weekends."

"That would be lovely," Wendy murmured.

"Then move there permanently once I retire."

"Hmm," Wendy agreed, but her eyebrows furrowed.

"And what exactly would we do there?" Wendy asked. "I'm not really versed in country living."

Walter laughed, "We'd hire that part out, obviously. We'd

enjoy the views, read books, travel," he said. "Live the good life."

Wendy smiled as he pulled her close. The good life. Sitting around and relaxing did sound wonderful, especially when juxtaposed with her current busyness running after two young boys. If this is all that life had to offer her—though it wasn't as exciting as she'd hoped—it was fulfilling in certain ways. She could be happy with a simpler life, couldn't she? Leaning her head on Walter's shoulder, she closed her eyes, listening to the happy shouts of the boys in the distance.

Chapter Thirty-Five

AUGUST, 2014

Walter woke the next morning to find Wendy still sound asleep next to him. The night before weighed heavily on his conscience, though he wasn't sure how to make it right. Especially because he didn't have complete control over fixing it. And it seemed that nothing he did lately could make things any better with Wendy, regardless.

He shifted his weight, lifting himself to a sitting position, and Wendy stirred next to him. Not wanting to wake her, he lifted his glasses from the nightstand, keeping his body as still as possible. Picking up his book, he scanned the page to pick up where he left off.

"Walter," Wendy said softly, turning over to face him.

He quickly set his book on his lap and took her in. He knew she wouldn't believe it if he told her, but he loved her face in the morning. Her rumpled hair, skin free of makeup or worries of the day. He hadn't spent enough time looking at her when he had the opportunity.

"Hmm?" he answered.

"I'm sorry about last night," she said, shifting to her side. "I was tired and emotionally drained."

"I think we both were," he said. "I'm sorry I chose a poor moment to express my thoughts."

When she didn't respond, he turned away. Lifting his book, he started reading, only to stop abruptly when he suddenly noticed Wendy again sniffling next to him.

"What's wrong?" he asked tentatively, this time fully putting his book away.

She didn't answer. Her face screwed up in anguish, and she clenched her jaw. Every part of her was stiff, as if damming the flood of emotions begging to be set free. Finally, she broke. Pulling her knees to her chest, she wrapped her arms around her legs and sobbed freely.

Elated at her unexpected vulnerability, Walter wanted more than anything to pull her close. Instead, he waited a moment, then spoke cautiously.

"I understand you don't want to be with me, but we *have* been together a long time. I know I haven't had a good track record of listening, and I'm so very sorry about that. But I'm here now, and I'd be happy to listen if you're willing to take that chance."

When Wendy was again silent, Walter knew he should probably let her be—get dressed and go down to the kitchen for breakfast—but he was tired of trying to do the right thing when it afforded him nothing. Opening his book for the third time, he slammed the door on all the 'shoulds' and stubbornly began to read.

He'd finished a chapter and a half before Wendy's voice broke his focus. She was breathing normally again and her voice was thin.

"I'm terrified," she whispered.

This time it was Walter's turn to stay silent. This felt...intimate. And desperate—as if intangible future moments hinged on this one. It made his heart begin to pound and his hands shake.

"I thought that if I broke free of all the things I felt restricted by over the years, I'd be happy," she continued, still clinging to her knees. "It was exciting to be in Paris—still is—but there's an...emptiness. It sounds ridiculous that I'm literally doing something I've always dreamed of, and I'm still not satisfied," she sighed in frustration. "Sometimes I think true happiness simply isn't in the cards for me."

"That's a little extreme, don't you think?" Walt said kindly.

"I dunno, is it?" she said desperately.

"Weren't you happy before? I mean back when things were going the way you wanted?" Walter asked, suddenly second guessing more than the past few years of their relationship.

"I think I probably was, but it was like I was just passing through. Getting married, raising kids, working, volunteering, all of it so I could someday 'arrive,' you know? One day find myself self-fulfilled and wise and all the things you're supposed to be when you get older. And then it...never happened. I think I'm lonely, Walt. I don't have any close friends—"

"You have Mary," he cut in.

"Even with Mary, it's not the same. There's so much drama, and it seems like we've different perspectives at the moment," she said, pausing. "I'm oversimplifying it, surely, but I haven't felt as excited to talk with her. I've truly felt lonely most of my life, I think. Then moving here...it put a magnifying glass on it."

Walter nodded, keeping his mouth closed even though his thoughts were spinning. Wendy hadn't ever made an effort to make friends. She never wanted to join him at work gatherings or community events. He was sure he'd suggested it years ago and hadn't gotten a good response. And how could she have felt lonely when he was always there? Her comments bit into him, needling the raw insecurities he'd only recently begun to wrestle with.

For the first time in his life, Walter was at a loss. Though there were times when he didn't tell someone how to solve their problem, he always had an idea in his mind of how they could. This time, he truly didn't know what the solution was. Wendy had been right about one thing: he didn't know her the way he thought he did. But it might be because she'd never let him—or anyone else—in.

"I wish I knew how to help," he said simply. "For me, life has felt less complicated, I think," he laughed wryly. "I do believe I'm capable of living differently than I have in the past, but you're right that I've always enjoyed stability and predictability. Following the same routine made me feel safe, and for me, safe is happy."

"But shouldn't happy be more than that?" Wendy postulated. "Isn't there more than just 'safe'?"

"These last few months I've felt very unsafe and I don't know that it's made me happier," he said, his voice building. "I've tried new things and been in situations that I never anticipated, and I'll admit, it has given me a sense of accomplishment, but happier?" he mused. "Wendy, remember when you talked about going big and really putting yourself out there?"

She nodded.

"Never in my life have I had the compulsion to do that!" he laughed. "And maybe that's why you feel like we're two totally different people. I've always just been...satisfied. I now know what you mean, though. It *was* thrilling to do something terrifying and come out mostly unscathed on the other side."

"This is exactly what I'm talking about," Wendy said, shifting her weight. "I didn't come out unscathed, Walter. I'm very, very...scathed!" she said, her tone lifting. "Why is it that you feel so—so solid and I'm—ugh! I don't know!" she said, tears welling in her eyes again.

"I don't know," Walter repeated, inhaling deeply. "There's quite possibly a lot less going on up here," he said, tapping his head. "Pros and cons, eh?" he laughed. "I'm not able to perceive my wife is living in a perpetual state of discontent, but I'm also not at risk of feeling dissatisfied in my own life."

Wendy rolled her eyes, "You're not an idiot, Walter."

"Well," he said, throwing his legs out from under the blankets and off the side of the bed, "that's up for debate."

He stepped to his suitcase and pulled out a fresh pair of clothes. "I'm in need of a shower before tackling everything waiting for us out there," he said, pointing past the door.

"Thank you," Wendy said before he could grip the door handle.

Walter stopped.

"For listening," she said.

He nodded his head, then opened the door and stepped into the hall.

Chapter Thirty-Six

"It's good to see you out and about," Wendy said, greeting Becky as she entered the kitchen. "How're you feeling?"

Becky shrugged, and Wendy took her cue, deciding to avoid badgering her with more questions.

"I've made scotch eggs and fried chicken," she said, placing the last drumstick on a plate and setting the tongs on the granite countertop.

"Thank you," Becky said, a wan smile on her lips.

"Smells amazing," Calvin said, walking in to join them. "Dad and I got the leak fixed on the faucet."

"Wow, that was nice of him," Becky said, sitting on one of the bar stools at the counter.

Wendy set the steaming plate of chicken in front of her, then pulled four plates and four cups from the cabinet.

"Your mom's been hard at work, too," Becky added.

"I can see that," Calvin said, standing behind his wife and wrapping his arms around her shoulders.

This simple physical contact was enough to fill Becky's eyes to the brim with fresh tears. She quickly swept them away, then picked up a plate. Walter entered the kitchen and immediately walked to the sink to wash his hands.

"Mum, Dad, I shouldn't've been so harsh last night," Calvin said, his hands resting on Becky's shoulders.

"Don't fret," Wendy said, placing sliced apples, forks, and napkins next to the plates. "We were all a little on edge."

Calvin nodded. "Thanks for being here."

Wendy smiled. "Shall we?"

After lunch, they all sat in the living room.

"How long before you go back to work?" Walter asked gently.

"I'll go back on Monday," Calvin said, then motioned for Becky to answer.

"I'm not sure yet. Physically, I could start tomorrow, but I can't decide if it would be best to take another week off...I don't know. It might be good to have a distraction."

"You could try it out and if you need more time, you could take it," Calvin said.

"I know," she nodded, "I just don't necessarily want to drag my co-workers through this."

"As far as financials, is your insurance taking care of everything?"

"Yep, we're all good there. Honestly, this whole thing could've been a lot worse in so many ways. Becky's health, for example...if the pregnancy would've gone on much longer, she could have been in a much more dangerous position."

Wendy nodded. "As hard as this is, we're so glad you're healthy," she said.

"Is there anything else I can do for you before I head home?" Walter asked.

"What time's your flight?" Calvin asked.

"I booked it for Sunday morning—ten o'clock."

"What about you, Mum?"

"I haven't booked it yet. I figured I'd see what you needed and go from there. If you'd like me to stay and keep you company next week, I'd be happy to stay a few days," Wendy offered.

"That's nice, thank you," Becky said. "I'll talk it over with Cal. If I go back to work Monday, I wouldn't want to make you stay for nothing."

"Just let me know," Wendy said, folding her hands in her lap.

"If you'd like, we could all go to this little Korean place a few blocks up for dinner. I know I'd like a nap this afternoon, but then we could go for a walk? Get some fresh air?"

"A nap sounds lovely," Walter said.

"I might sneak out and do a little shopping while you all rest," Wendy said.

"Reconvene here at three-thirty?" Calvin said, standing and pulling Becky from the sofa.

Wendy nodded, then reached for her purse.

Chapter Thirty-Seven

Opening the door to her flat, Wendy stumbled through the door and collapsed on the chair in the living room. It was only ten in the morning Paris time, which felt like a particularly cruel fact. With her delayed flight, she'd been stuck at Heathrow overnight and had found it impossible to get more than a couple hours of sleep on her first flight out of SFO. Her body hungered for rest, but she knew well enough that if she allowed herself a small nap, that hour would easily turn into six, and then she'd be awake—alone—all night long.

Forcing herself to stand, she pulled her wallet and phone from her travel bag and looked for a smaller bag. Pulling her leather purse from the shelf next to her bed, she tossed in her belongings and walked to the door in search of a late breakfast and a large dose of caffeine.

With dragging feet, she walked into the cafe, placed her order and reached into her bag for payment. As she did so, she felt something foreign next to her wallet. She pulled out the stiff paper and her brow furrowed. She definitely hadn't seen this pale yellow envelope before, nor had she put it in her purse. This bag had been sitting in Paris while she was at Calvin's, so it couldn't have been from him—though that would've been sweet had he written her a thank-you note.

The man behind the counter cleared his throat, and Wendy hurriedly pulled out her wallet with her free hand, set the envelope on the counter, and pulled out her Visa. When it was approved, she tucked it into her wallet and nodded a quick 'merci' before pulling the envelope back into her hand. Turning it over, she walked toward the window and slumped into a chair.

She ripped it open. Inside she found a piece of stationary with daisies floating whimsically along the edges. Her eyes moved to the greeting, and she began to read.

Wendy,

I'm not sure when you'll see this, but I assume it will be sooner rather than later. You've always been one for details, so I'm sure this won't escape your notice for long.

She flipped the paper over to identify the sender. Walter. How long ago had he put this in her bag? The last time she remembered using it was at the museum. Had he—? Quickly turning it back to the beginning, she continued on.

I can't properly describe my feelings as I write this. Mostly because I've had very little practice with expressing emotions (as you well know) but also because I'm not sure they've settled into anything coherent. It's kind of 'everything all mixed into one big blob' at the moment. If I had to choose a word, it would be 'incredibly overwhelmed.' That's two words, I know. Close enough.

I'm 'incredibly overwhelmed' by my regret, which has led to a surprising amount of self-loathing. I'm also 'incredibly overwhelmed' by my gratitude for the life we've had, even though it clearly wasn't perfect. I'm 'incredibly overwhelmed' at having to shift my expectations for the future. That one seems the hardest, by far. It seems that every hour I'm finding a new thing to be lost. Another picture of how my life would look over the next ten or twenty years completely altered.

I don't say this to inflict pain or guilt, but merely to be honest. And to selfishly provoke a bit of compassion from you as we navigate what will surely be some difficult waters moving forward.

In one of our first conversations back in May, you ruminated on what love really is. I remember you asking the question: "shouldn't it be more?" I'll be honest, I don't have much experience with love (as you also know), but being married for twenty-eight years should at least qualify me for some sort of comment, eh?

I've felt very loved by you, Wendy. I know now that I didn't do a good job of showing it, but I did. I felt loved when you woke each morning and prepared me breakfast. When I came home to a warm dinner. When you took such care in nurturing our children. When you took an interest in the struggles I had at work or asked me questions about the programs I was watching on the telly.

I felt loved, but as I write that list, each item is like a blow to my being because I know I didn't put forth the same effort to take care of you or get to know you. It wasn't because I didn't love. It was because I didn't know differently. All I'd seen was what seemed to be good enough for my parents, so that's what I did. That's what I thought a man was supposed to do. It's laugh-

able, honestly, but I never questioned it. I'm so sorry I never questioned it.

Thank you for shaking me out of tradition and helping me recognize that in myself. I'm truly sorry, Wendy. I can't seem to say that enough.

But, I'm sure you're sick of hearing it, so on to something else. As I make my way back home, I couldn't help but leave you with a few ideas for your continued time in Paris. I'd made a list of future dates for the two of us and couldn't stand the thought of such effort being wasted. I do hope you'll enjoy some of them and that one day, when things are a bit brighter, you can tell me what you liked best.

Love Walter

Wendy wiped a tear from her cheek and scanned the list below his signature. See a movie at La Pagode. Spend the morning at Le Marché de Belleville. She'd heard of that market, but hadn't made it to the Eleventh Arrondissement to see what the fuss was about. Everything on his list—all fifteen items—sounded perfectly wonderful.

Folding the paper back up, she replaced it gently in its envelope. A server arrived with her breakfast and she gratefully took a bite of her pastry as soon as he turned back to the counter. She gazed out the window, only half-watching the passers-by as the warm butter and sugar melted on her tongue.

Chapter Thirty-Eight

SEPTEMBER, 2014

Walter Winslow stared at the papers in front of him. It had only been two weeks since they'd been at Calvin's and Becky's, but it seemed like much longer. Wendy had called once to let him know Ms. Statterly would be sending the divorce paperwork. He hadn't said much and therefore the conversation didn't last long. At the time, he'd wondered if Wendy had thought any more about life and happiness, but hadn't found a proper way to ask her without seeming overly invested. Even though he was.

He'd stared at this particular envelope for at least four days, but had finally ripped off the bandage that morning. Now, almost past feeling, he turned the page and placed his signature on the line. He did this three more times, the blue ink from his pen slipping onto the parchment effortlessly, as if this wasn't the official end of life as Walter knew it. He'd done everything he could, hadn't he? Wendy would've had him signing this months ago had he not fought for more time.

They had written a contract and he had agreed to the terms. Which meant...

He quickly stuffed the paperwork into a new, postmarked envelope that had been included in the first and sealed it closed. Then, snatching his jacket from the coat-rack just in case, he headed out the door to the post office to drop off the package as soon as it opened. After this task was complete, he could get on with his Saturday as usual. The yard needed mowing and the raspberries needed picking. All he had to do was run this quick, harmless errand and everything could go back to normal.

Later that day, Walter knelt on the grass and reached gloved hands underneath the rose bush to pull two thistles that had somehow escaped his notice earlier in the week. As he resurfaced victoriously, someone cleared their throat behind him and he turned, startled.

"Wendy," he said in shock. "What on earth are you doing here?"

"When we were in Paris," she said, "I saw you."

"Yes...I saw you, too," Walter said slowly.

"No, I mean—I saw you after you told me you'd be heading home. I saw you that day on the street—outside the cafe."

Walter's eyebrows furrowed as he searched his memory. "I'm not sure—"

"You were canoodling with some woman you'd never mentioned. She had grey hair, very classy—"

Walter held up his hands. "First of all, Genevieve and I were not 'canoodling'," he said, immediately on the defensive, based on Wendy's choice of words. "She was—*is*—a friend. And a much-needed one, at that. We'd been meeting for brunch a couple of times a week."

Wendy's face turned an angry color of red as she processed this information. "Why didn't you tell me you'd met someone? Here I thought—"

"Thought what? That I'd be sitting alone in my flat just waiting for the unlikely occasion when you'd actually want to spend time with me?"

"Ah," Wendy scoffed, rolling her eyes.

"What do you expect from me, Wendy? Did you honestly travel all the way to Colorado to pick a fight?"

"No, I—"

"That week, you made it unequivocally clear that you had no intention of changing your mind regarding the divorce. Did you want me to hole up in my flat feeling sorry for myself? Grieving—*for the rest of my life*—the relationship I lost by being too clueless and selfish?"

Wendy's brow furrowed and she stood very still.

"I've done my grieving! In case you haven't noticed, living alone in a city I barely knew wasn't exactly a walk in the park for an old codger like me. Even though you talk now about feeling lonely, it seemed at the time like you'd built a fairly well-rounded life there. But for me? It wasn't that easy. So yes, I was eating brunch with my friend Genevieve."

Wendy stared at the floor in silence.

Walter breathed heavily, wondering what in the world had come over him. No 'hi, hello, Wendy!' just your average verbal barrage for someone he hadn't seen in weeks? To be fair, she had started with an inflammatory question...

"Walt..." Wendy spoke finally, mustering her courage. "What if—what if...I was wrong."

"About Genevieve? On that one you've just about lost the plot."

Wendy's eyes flashed. "I'm sorry I led with that," she said in a less than apologetic tone, "but you have to admit, it didn't exactly look innocent—"

"Perhaps to you—"

"Perhaps to anyone who didn't know the whole story," she insisted. "I came here to do this and realized I needed to know what that was. It was eating at me, you know?" she prattled on, so fast that Walter had trouble taking in her words.

"I thought about ignoring it, but I knew it would cause problems for me, and then—if I waited too long—that would be strange and awkward to bring it up later—"

"Wendy!" Walter stopped her, pulling the gloves from his hands and tossing them on the lawn. "What is 'this' exactly?"

"What d'you mean?" she asked.

"You just said 'I came here to do this'—?"

"Right," she said, folding and unfolding her hands nervously. "Well. I found your letter."

Walter's eyes widened. "When?" he breathed.

"After I returned to Paris. After Calvin's."

"Ah," Walter said. "I assumed you'd already seen it," he said, shuffling his feet.

"No, I took that bag home after the museum and must have taken my wallet out without noticing it. I found a small backpack the day before we met up—it was at that flea market, you know the one just past the bus station on—" she searched for the street.

"I know the one," Walter said.

Wendy looked relieved, the name still escaping her. "I didn't use that purse again until I got back."

Walter nodded.

"You remembered I love daisies."

"Why do you think I grow them?" Walter said, gesturing toward a clump of flowers near the step.

"Because I bought the seeds," Wendy teased.

Reddening slightly, Walter muttered, "Well I still planted them, didn't I?"

"It doesn't matter," Wendy said, trying to avoid another

distraction. "I came here to say: what if I was wrong—not about your friend, whatever-her-name-is. Wrong about *this*," she explained, gesturing to the space between them.

Walter cocked his head, befuddled. "The yard?"

Wendy sighed in exasperation. "Walt, what if I was wrong about—going to Paris! About splitting up! The whole thing!"

Walter pondered this a moment. "I guess...I'm not following. Do you wish we would've signed the papers and not gone to Paris? It could've saved a lot of money, that's for sure—"

"Walter!" Wendy shrieked. "I was searching for something —something big—to make me happy. To force me into this fulfillment I've been missing. But every amazing thing I saw in Paris didn't fill that void! It did for the moment, I guess, but then I'd end up at my apartment feeling emptier than I had before I left. I still don't know what I want, and I'm positive I'm quite emotionally unstable at the moment. I might change my mind tomorrow, but...I think I might...a wee bit...*perhaps* care about you," she said, biting her lip. "I think I was wrong about us," she continued. "I don't want to get a divorce—quite yet, at least—and I just—I just want to be *home*," she finished, her eyes welling with tears.

A look of complete shock passed over Walter's face and Wendy wondered for the briefest of moments whether he was about to suffer a heart attack.

"Walt?" she said softly.

In one swift movement, Walter threw his sunhat on the grass with his gloves and closed the gap between them, pulling her into his arms. Without saying a word, he kissed her. He kissed her with a passion he hadn't ever experienced. When they first fell in love, their kisses were full of desire and excitement, but not this. This feeling was full-bodied and rich with experience. Deepened by the hurt and anguish of struggle and perceived loss, followed by the joy of potential and renewed vulnerability. That afternoon in his own backyard, Walter Winslow kissed his wife as he had never kissed anyone before.

As he pulled away, Wendy's eyes were wide and she clung to his arm to avoid wobbling on her unsteady legs.

"There's one slight problem," Walter said, and Wendy's eyes flicked to his. "I've just sent in my signed divorce papers."

"I called Ms. Statterly two days ago. I told her I'd be waiting to sign mine."

"What did she say?" Walter questioned.

"She asked if your contract worked," Wendy laughed timidly.

"What did you tell her?"

"That it failed. Miserably."

Walter laughed out-loud. "It was terrible, wasn't it?"

"Wonderful at times...and yes, surprisingly terrible," Wendy agreed.

A thought occurred to Walter, and he stepped back so he could see his wife clearly. "Do you think...we could make another one?"

"Another what?" she asked skeptically, noticing the glint of mischief in his eye.

"Another contract. You know, try again."

"In Paris?" she asked.

"Perhaps," Walter shrugged.

"We'd...try again...again...in Paris?" she said, laughing at the ridiculousness of it.

"Why not? You've said you don't know who you are or if you can be happy, and I still need to learn to be flexible, which means I need something to get me out of my routine every once in a while. I'm not saying I can leave the office right away—"

"But maybe next summer?" she suggested. "And I'm not saying this is all hunky-dory," she said, taking a step back, her tone serious. "I didn't say divorce was off the table completely—"

"Just that you'd like more time to think about it," Walter repeated.

"Right," she nodded stubbornly.

"Next summer could work. Between now and then, I could write you more letters," he said cheekily.

She smiled briefly at his comment, but then Wendy's face fell. "Walt...I'm serious about what I said. I'm worried I still might not be able to figure this out," she said nervously. "What if I still feel this—itch to get out and do something different?"

"Then we'll scratch it together," he said, realizing too late the odd metaphor he'd created. Wendy wrinkled her nose, and they both laughed.

"Wendy Winslow," Walter said formally, taking a knee and reaching for her hand. "I'm not sure what my future will hold—though I'm positive it will include more hair loss and aggravating aches and pains—but I'm one-hundred percent certain I want you in it."

Wendy's eyes welled with tears at the gesture, remembering the moment he proposed so many years ago.

"Will you join me," Walter continued, "in trying again...again?"

"I'll try my very best," Wendy said, "I promise."

Standing, Walter wrapped his arms around his wife of twenty-eight years and squeezed her tight. Later that night, he'd check off the very last item written on the list that still hung on his wall. 'Believe you can be whole again.' As Wendy's head rested on his chest, he didn't need to believe. He knew.

The End

About the Author

Cynthia Gunderson is best known for her award-winning and best-selling novel, Yes, And. She has written nine full-length novels, as well as two children's series under the pen names Cindy Gunderson (sci-fi) and Cindy Prince (children's).

When she is not writing in a quiet corner of her local library, you can find her traveling with her family, recording audiobooks, or happily digging in her garden.

Cynthia grew up in Alberta, Canada, but has lived most of her adult life between California and Colorado. She currently resides in the Denver metro area with her four children and handsome husband, Scott. Cindy holds a B.S. in Psychology from Brigham Young University. She teaches regularly at writer's conferences around the country.

Also by Cynthia Gunderson

Yes, And

Holly Bough Cottage

The New Year's Party

www.CindyGunderson.com

Instagram: @CindyGWrites

Facebook: @CindyGWrites

TikTok: @CynthiaGWrites

Made in the USA
Columbia, SC
04 March 2023

13230262R00117